"What's in this for you?" Sonny asked.

"I take your brother back to the U.S. for prosecution before the bail needs to be paid and I get a nice bonus for my troubles," Gil said. "That's the way it works."

"Me and the baby, too?" she asked. "Do you take us, too?"

The words were out of her mouth before she even had time to comprehend what she'd said. The surprise in his eyes mirrored what she felt. But it was the only way. She'd come far, but she couldn't do this alone. She needed help and if she worked this right, she and Ellie might be able to get back to the States alive.

"Go on. Get in," he said quietly.

She closed her eyes and sighed softly, soothing the fussy baby in her arms.

Gil was after money. She was out of money. He wanted her brother. She wanted safety for all of them. She had only one choice, not that she liked it. She had to go with him. She stepped off the curb and into the back seat of the compact car, hoping she hadn't just made the biggest mistake of her life.

Books by Lisa Mondello

Love Inspired Suspense

Cradle of Secrets
Her Only Protector

LISA MONDELLO

Lisa's love of writing romance started early when she penned her first romance novel (a full fifty-eight pages long, but who's counting) at the age of ten. She then went on to write a mystery script that impressed her sixth grade teacher so much he let her and her friends present it as a play to the whole grade. There was no stopping her after that! After going to college for sound recording technology and managing a Boston rock band for four years, she settled down with her husband of over sixteen years and raised a family. Although she's held many jobs through the years, ranging from working with musicians and selling kitchen and catering tools to teaching first and second graders with special needs how to read and write, her love of writing has always stayed in the forefront, and she is now a full-time freelance writer. Lisa lives in western Massachusetts with her husband, four children (who never cease to amaze her as they grow), a very pampered beagle and a rag-doll cat who thinks she owns them all.

Lisa Mondello

Her Only PROTECTOR

Steeple
Hill®

Published by Steeple Hill Books™

STEEPLE HILL BOOKS

Steeple
Hill®

ISBN-13: 978-0-373-44303-1
ISBN-10:   0-373-44303-X

HER ONLY PROTECTOR

Copyright © 2008 by Lisa Mondello

www.SteepleHill.com

Printed in U.S.A.

Trust in the Lord forever, for in God the Lord, we have an everlasting rock.
—*Isaiah* 26:4

To all the men and women who risk their lives rescuing American-born children being held captive in foreign countries.

ONE

Sonny Montgomery had an itch she couldn't scratch. It sat dead center between her shoulder blades, just out of arm's reach. Like a persistent mosquito buzzing around her ear, it nagged at her. But she couldn't stop to deal with it. Even a small move like that could attract unwanted attention on these South American streets.

She needed to remain invisible. To be in and out of Colombia without anyone being able to recognize or remember her. Any connection to her family either by name or face would spell certain death for her and the baby.

And Cash. That is, if her brother was still alive. If the Colombian kingpin who had kidnapped Cash's baby girl from her cradle in Eastmeadow, Massachusetts, just four months ago had shown him enough mercy not to kill him. But she couldn't think about that. The Lord had brought her this far on her journey. She had to trust that He would help Cash with his.

She held tight to the basket of fruit—it was heavy and her arm ached. She focused her mind on the ache instead of all she couldn't control. Slipping her free hand beneath her poncho, she checked to make sure that her traveling papers were still in her money belt, which was strapped to her waist. They were.

Thanks to the duplicate passport the U.S. Embassy had issued for the baby, they'd both be able to fly out of Colombia without incident. Hopefully. The Colombian government might challenge it. But she was ready to deal with that if it happened.

Sonny was having a hard time coming to terms with what she was doing. Never in her life had she entertained the idea of doing anything illegal. And here she was in Colombia, ready to steal a baby and flee to the United States.

But it was the only way. Even her brother, Dylan, a former marine and a Chicago cop, had assured her of that. Off the record, of course.

It had rained in the night and the pungent smell of mud, earth and rotting garbage permeated the quiet, early-morning streets. A thick mist drifted up from the already hot ground. In an hour, the fruit market in the center of the city would be open. Some of the street vendors were already setting up their carts full of goods, ready for the tourists who would soon crowd the road, eager to barter for a bargain.

It was a long walk from her little room near the foothills to the center of town. It was also a dangerous walk so early in the morning, alone. But escaping the city would be much easier if she didn't have to contend with the morning traffic.

If all went well, Sonny would be long gone by the morning rush. And any evidence of her trip to Colombia would be erased. The team would make sure of that.

They had her back—Dylan had promised her. *Lord, I hope so.*

Closing her eyes for a brief moment, she ran through her part of the plan one more time, telling herself she had to get it right. There was no room for error. The sooner she had the baby in her care and was out of Colombia and away from Eduardo Sanchez, the head of the Aztec Corporation, the sooner she'd be able to relax. Really relax. Not like the falling-down-because-you-can't-stay-awake-anymore type of relaxing she'd been doing since she'd first learned her niece had been kidnapped by the Colombian businessman involved in organized crime.

The sweat of her palm made it hard to hold the heavy wicker basket in her hand, but she gripped it tighter, ignoring the urge to stretch her arm and scratch her back. As moisture beaded on her brow, Sonny thanked God for the ache in her arm and the itch between her shoulder blades. They kept her mind off her nerves. Off all the things that could go wrong in a long string of choreographed steps that had to be perfectly performed in order for the plan to work.

She thought of her brother. Cash would have been as against her coming to Colombia as Dylan had been at first. But then, both of them wanted to believe she was still their baby sister tagging along behind them and not the capable twenty-five-year-old woman she'd grown into. Cash hadn't noticed much of her maturing since he'd become an agent for the Drug Enforcement Administration. Dylan, the eldest, had missed even more while he was away in the military. If it weren't for the fact that she was the only person who could make this plan work, she'd probably be padlocked in her bedroom.

But Sonny couldn't think about Cash or Dylan right now. The baby was her only concern. If she failed…

No. I'm not leaving this country without little Ellie.

She walked off the path and onto the paved road, leading to the center of the city. Unlike the outskirts of town, central Monteria was modern, much like an American city. Stores and restaurants catered to the foreign tourist. Concrete high-rise hotels and office buildings packed the downtown streets. It seemed almost strange that a city like this could be just a few hundred meters from foothills that were lush with greenery and jungle.

The basket of fruit she held was just a prop, a reason for her to be walking the streets at this hour of the morning should anyone take notice of her. She'd learned that only vendors walked the road this early in the morning. She couldn't risk renting a car or calling for a taxi—that would leave evidence of where she'd been and where she was going.

If she checked her watch, it would confirm what the sky was telling her now as light kissed the horizon and chased away the darkness from the alleyways and side streets. Her pulse pounded as the light grew brighter, the shadows stretching and then fading away. Blood raced through her veins so quickly she was sure her heart was about to burst in her chest.

It was almost time.

She was ready. As ready as she could be. She'd told Lucia she'd meet her two streets over from the market-place. The road provided easy access in and out of the city. They'd avoid early marketplace crowds and the eyes of anyone who might be watching.

As she rounded the corner and reached the meeting place, she paused just a fraction of a second and listened. The urgent whine of a car engine and tires screeching cut into the calm of the morning. She checked her watch and then looked up to see a bright red blur speeding toward her, the noise of dirty spark plugs sputtering at an ear-splitting volume.

So much for being covert.

They were earlier than she expected. "Thank you, Lord," she whispered.

The dusty compact car ground to a halt next to her.

"Get in!" the driver demanded as he reached across the seat and threw open the passenger side door. Sonny knew the black-haired man in his early fifties as Torres. She had only met him once. All other contact had been made through his contact at the marketplace and his daughter, Lucia.

"Is it done?" she asked quickly.

"Leave the basket," he ordered in a commanding voice made harsher by his thick accent. "You must get in, Sonia!"

Sonny jumped into action, unaccustomed to the use of her given name. Stepping off the curb, she caught sight of a figure slumped over in the backseat with a bright red blood stain spreading across a white shirt. She couldn't see the face, but she knew who it was.

Heart in her throat, she gasped, "Oh, dear Lord, no! No! Lucia?"

"Get in, I tell you! Do you want us all to be killed?" Sonny dropped the basket, the contents spilling over the potholed street. She hadn't even shut the door before the wheels of the vehicle started spinning again.

Sweat poured off Torres's forehead and his hands trembled so violently he couldn't still them on the steering wheel. It didn't take a genius to figure out one of the delicate steps in their plan had gone terribly wrong.

Oh, God. Where's Ellie? Please not Ellie. She's just a little baby.

Despite the speed of the car flying through the narrow streets, Sonny abandoned the idea of putting on her seat belt and reached into the backseat to touch Lucia. The stench of blood overwhelmed the car.

"Is she…"

Torres kept his eyes on the road. "Leave her."

"But she needs help!" Sonny protested, tears stinging her eyes. "We need to help her."

"Nothing can be done. She's dead. I'll take care of her body later."

In horror, Sonny swallowed the bile making its way up her throat. She fought to find her voice. Then swallowed again. *Torres's daughter was dead.*

"The baby?" she asked, choking back a sob. "Ellie?"

"Asleep under the shawl. Leave her be. She'll be fine and no one will notice us as long as you turn around and act normal."

"How is that possible?" There was so much blood. Sonny fought the urge to check Lucia just to see if Torres was wrong. *Oh, please, God, let him be wrong.* She forced herself to turn around and slip on her seat belt.

The older man glanced at her. "We need to get out of the city and to the airport right away."

Sonny stole a quick glance over her shoulder at the bundle next to Lucia's body and closed her eyes to keep the tears at bay. She had the baby now. This was exactly what she'd come here to do. But the image of Lucia's blood-stained body was imprinted in her mind and she wondered if the price of getting the baby had been too high. For Lucia and Torres, it had.

When she trusted her voice again, she asked, "What went wrong?"

"Nothing," Torres said, his voice flat. "The extraction happened exactly as planned."

"I don't understand."

"An old debt has been repaid. We make enemies doing what we do. Lucia knew that. This had nothing to do with you or your family."

Torres reached across the small confines of the car and pushed his rough palm against Sonny's cheek with a force that hurt. "Hide your face."

An oncoming police car sped toward them, lights flashing. She quickly turned her gaze to the floor. The car hit a pothole and she gripped the dash with both hands for support.

When the police car passed, she glanced back. "Do you think they were after us?"

"No."

"How can you be sure?"

Torres didn't answer and when Sonny finally looked at him again, it broke her heart to see the man's weary eyes steeped in pain, his weathered face momentarily contorted with grief.

He cleared his throat. "Do you still have them?"

"What?"

"The papers! Do you have the papers with you?" he

said, his voice raspy. "We can't waste time going back to the hotel to get them or to make new ones."

"Yes. I have them. I was able to get the passport for the baby."

"Good. Your only concern now is to get on that plane back to your country. When you get to the airport buy some new clothes, get rid of what you have here and stay out of sight until you board. Don't let anything stand in the way of getting on that plane. When you and Ellie are safe, the sacrifice my daughter made will be worthwhile."

He was right, she knew. But his words did nothing to dispel the guilt consuming her. She had begged them for help, and now Lucia was dead. She had caused Torres and his family this pain.

Lucia had a son of her own who was barely four years old, she'd told Sonny on their first meeting. And a husband who disapproved of what she was trying to do. Yet Lucia had agreed to help rescue Ellie anyway.

Sonny'd had no choice in asking for their help, of course. She'd been desperate to find any information about the whereabouts of her niece and was thrilled when her online digging expedition led her to information about the head of the Aztec Corporation's new baby.

A computer geek by trade, trained to hack into computer systems for large companies to ensure security or expose weaknesses, Sonny had found the proverbial needle in the haystack that led her to Ellie. No one, not even those close to Eduardo Sanchez, willingly questioned why an American baby had suddenly arrived in a Colombian home. With so many American families waiting to adopt, it seemed unlikely that a legal adoption had taken place.

Yet no one was willing to publicly question how this baby came to be. Not if they wanted to continue breathing.

Sonny closed her eyes, fighting her desire to take the baby out of the backseat and into her arms. She wanted so much to hold Ellie, to look at her for the first time. Make sure she was all right.

Did she have Cash's smile or her sister-in-law, Serena's, exotic look? Did she still cry for her mother? It had been so long since Sonny learned that Ellie had been taken from the mansion in Eastmeadow, Massachusetts. And yet here was Ellie now, sleeping soundly in the backseat of the car.

She is safe there. No one can see her sleeping in the backseat. No one can hurt her. She just has to hold on a little longer. Instead of cradling the precious girl against her chest to tell her that she was going to a safe home filled with love, Sonny said a silent prayer of thanks to the Lord for seeing them both safely through this far. And another prayer for Lucia, that she would find peace with her heavenly Father.

Gil's stomach was growling. The pretzels he'd eaten half an hour ago hadn't done much for him. He needed a hot shower, a good meal and about three days' worth of solid sleep. None of that was likely to happen until he caught Cash Montgomery, brought him back to the States and collected his fee from the bail bondsman.

Well, maybe he'd get a shower. He should. If he had

any chance of getting close to Cash's sister, Sonny, he'd do better not to offend her with a rank smell.

The woman knew where her brother was. Gil was sure of it. And now she was on the run.

He'd been watching her every move for the past three weeks. He'd been right to follow her down to Colombia. Her brother was an agent with the DEA who'd turned, probably when the smell of money got too good.

It happened for a lot of reasons that Gil didn't really care about. Montgomery got his hand caught in the cookie jar and would have to pay his due. He'd given Cash's sister some room, sure that she was going to lead Gil right to his bounty. But for some reason, she'd holed up in a hotel room, barely leaving except to get food at the market.

Vacation? No way. Not in that low-class hotel. Who came down here and hid out in a place like that unless they were up to something? The woman was a computer geek, not a novelist who needed "space."

He'd gone to her hotel room this morning only to find it empty. And now she was boarding a plane back to the States.

Nope. Not going to happen. Not if Gil could help it. If Cash Montgomery was here in Colombia, Sonny was going to help Gil find him.

The whole time he'd been watching her hotel room, something had nagged at him. He'd heard of informants hanging around at the market under the pretense of being legitimate vendors. "Here's your oranges, *senoritas,* and oh, by the way your brother is hiding…"

Maybe. Maybe not. Gil was the proud owner of an overactive imagination. His creative—but critical—

thinking had gotten him far in his quests for justice. He'd earned the respect of his peers many times over when he brought a criminal back in the final hour—and earned pretty big rewards, too. Marco, one of the members of the small team he worked with to capture fugitives, was still talking about the payout on the job they did in San Juan as if Bill Gates had died and left all his money to Team Gil.

Yeah, okay. The bounty had been big, but it wasn't enough to retire on. The Cash Montgomery bounty would bring in a lot more than San Juan.

Gil chuckled at the irony of the fugitive's name, wondering just how much cash Cash was worth. In some ways, he hated thinking in terms of money, but it was necessary if he was ever going to leave bounty hunting behind. He wasn't retiring anytime soon, but finding Cash Montgomery was at least going to pay for a well-deserved vacation on some tropical island. A nice breezy cabana was just the ticket. Maybe he'd even rent one of those catamarans and go scuba diving for sunken treasure.

He was good at what he did but was in serious need of down time—he'd been chasing criminals for far too long.

Gil watched the women's room door, waiting for movement. He'd seen Sonny Montgomery go into the bathroom fifteen minutes ago. She'd probably been told to stay out of sight until her flight. If he were helping her to lay low, that's what he'd tell her to do.

The clock on the wall let him know her flight to the United States was going to start boarding in about fifteen minutes, but she hadn't even gone through security yet. He saw that there was virtually no one in line—she'd make it through security quickly. By his calculations, she should be showing her face any second now in order to make her flight with no time to spare.

He gave her points for that, too. She'd been coached well by someone who knew how to stay covert. He'd have to move fast if he planned on stopping her.

"Whoa," he said, pushing his sunglasses up to see if his eyes were playing tricks on him as she emerged from the bathroom.

Gil had expected Sonny to come out of the bathroom wearing the same poncho he'd seen her in all week. He'd almost missed her when she emerged wearing a very American jacket and blue jeans. Strapped around her front was a baby carrier, complete with a baby in tow. The only thing missing from this happy home-maker picture was a husband.

How sweet.

Words crackled in Spanish over the loudspeaker above his head, announcing the flight was about to board. His Spanish was good, but not as good as his cohorts, Cooper and Marco—he usually let them handle interpretation. But he'd heard the same announcement with different destinations for the past hour and after the second time, he figured out what it was saying. What else did he have to do while staking out the bathroom?

As Sonny walked by him, she kept her eyes fixed straight ahead and her body rigid. Even when he came up alongside her, she didn't so much as twitch.

Bad move. Even a cursory glance would have been more natural. It was less suspicious to anyone who might be watching.

"Cute kid," he said, grabbing her lightly by the arm. "Why don't we take a stroll over to the window so we can have a nice private conversation?"

Her face was stricken, filled with the panic of a trapped animal as she pulled her arm away from him. "I don't have any money. Nothing valuable. Please let go of me."

"Not a chance, lady."

"If you don't leave me alone, I'll scream."

"You don't really want to do that. You see those guards over there? Mikey Machine Gun and Sammy Soldier are looking a little bored with nothing to do but watch all the nice tourists go by hour after hour. I'm sure they'll be only too happy to take some time out of their busy schedules to ask how you acquired a baby on your little visit down here to their fine country."

Her face drained of blood and turned a stark white. "Please don't do this. I beg of you. You don't know what you're doing."

"Wrong. I know exactly what I'm doing, Ms. Montgomery." Her eyes widened with the use of her name. Although he'd been sure, confirmation that he'd been tailing the right woman was nice. He'd hate to find out he'd wasted all this time tailing the wrong girl.

With his hand still on her arm, he gave a quick glance to the soldiers, who were indeed more than a little curious at their sudden interaction.

"Act like you know me," he said in a low voice.

He didn't really need the Colombian police interfering in his business, either. That would only complicate matters since he was way out of his jurisdiction. They had their own kind of law down here and they didn't always care about what was deemed legal in the U.S.

Of course, Sonny Montgomery didn't need to know that.

"What?"

"Pretend you know me," he insisted quietly. Then in a louder voice he said, "Baby, I'm only a little late getting here. I told you I was sorry about last night. You don't have to be so angry with me. No harm done."

The light in her eyes flared. "What are you doing?"

He lowered his voice, his lips barely moving. "If you don't want to be detained and questioned by these officers for hours on end, follow my lead."

She shook her head. "No. I won't go with you."

"Sweetie, don't be sore and leave. Our vacation isn't even over yet. Let's have some fun."

His heart rate kicked up a notch when he noticed their little altercation was indeed stirring real interest from the gun boys. Sammy Soldier's finger had already moved into position on that bad-looking gun strapped around his shoulder.

"You don't have any idea of what you're doing," she whispered, her voice cracking. "I need to get on that plane right now."

"And I need to find your brother. You remember him, right? Cash? He needs to come clean or he'll owe my boss a cool million when he finally shows his face."

He hadn't expected her reaction. Panic, yes. Defiance, most definitely. Her brother was on the run and everything he'd uncovered about Sonny Montgomery was that she was tight with her family. He hadn't expected her wide-eyed expression of…hope?

"Do you know where Cash is?" she asked desperately.

He shook off the feeling that looking into her big deep blue eyes gave him. They were the color of the ocean with little flecks of green and gold that sparkled unlike anything he'd ever seen. She'd changed her hair—curled it somehow, making it more sophisticated than the pulled-back style she'd favored these past few days. Or maybe it was just the heat and humidity.

He laughed, mostly to pull his gaze away from the slight tilt of her nose and the intense way her eyes were now peering at him.

"Yeah, right."

"Tell me. You know where he is. Tell me where I can find my brother."

Sonny couldn't believe the break. Okay, it was the absolute *wrong* time for her to be just standing there in the middle of the airport, but if this man knew anything about Cash, she had to find out. Dylan could use the information to find him. She hated that she hadn't had any contact with Dylan since she'd come down to Colombia—she had no idea if he'd succeeded in finding Cash on his own.

They called her flight again. She glanced at the security checkpoint. Lucia had specifically told her to book this flight at this time because there would be less of a wait in the security line. If this man didn't get out of her way fast, she wouldn't make it in time to board her flight.

The voice on the loudspeaker spoke in Spanish first and then English. "Last call for all passengers boarding flight 1031 for Miami, Florida."

"I have to get on that plane," she said. "Please, tell me what you know now. I need to go."

"You're not going anywhere. I need *you* to tell *me* where your brother is." The man tightened his grip on her arm.

Her heart plummeted to the floor. He didn't know. And now, she was wasting precious time by standing here with him.

She quashed her disappointment as Ellie stirred in her carrier. She was probably hungry. But until they were in the air, Sonny wouldn't be able to do anything to satisfy her.

"Let go of me," she said. "Can't you see you're upsetting my baby?"

"*Your* baby? Right." The man muttered something harsh under his breath as he eyed the guards. "Terrific. We have company."

One of the guards was approaching them. His gun looked old and dusty, but deadly just the same. She knew there was little tolerance for Americans in Colombia. The government wanted their money and tourism, but there were stories of people coming for vacation and vanishing into thin air.

It was a miracle that they'd been able to find the baby at all. But if word got out that Ellie was the baby taken from Eduardo Sanchez's estate, Sonny was as good as dead—and no one back home would be the wiser.

At first, she'd questioned whether the baby in her arms was really Cash's daughter. Cash had been so secretive about his life leading up to the time of his arrest and disappearance. It had been a surprise for Sonny's whole family to find out that Cash had secretly married and had a baby girl who had been abducted by Eduardo

Sanchez. After the shock had worn off, they all knew what they had to do. They had to rescue both Cash and Ellie.

Even with all the information they'd been able to find about Eduardo Sanchez, there were many times during the long wait in that dingy hotel room in Monteria that Sonny fought with the notion she might be kidnapping a baby from her rightful parents. The thought of bringing pain to someone else was too much to bear.

But once Sonny had gotten over the shock of Lucia's death and pushed the poncho off the basket with the sleeping baby inside, she knew. One look at the child and she saw her mother. This baby was a Montgomery through and through, and Sonny knew there was no turning back. She had to make sure Ellie made it back to the United States. Back to Cash and his wife, Serena.

The guard's voice was commanding as he yelled at them in Spanish.

"I'm sorry. We were just leaving," the stranger said, turning his attention away from her but keeping his hand firmly in place on her arm.

The guard looked vicious as he shouted at them again. It was hard to keep up with the fast-paced Colombian dialect but Sonny got the gist of it. He wanted them to state their business. She could talk to them—tell them that this man was keeping her from getting on her plane—but would they just detain her further while sorting it all out?

And what about the baby? She really didn't want them to ask any questions about Ellie.

Oh, Lord, please help me through this. Help me figure out how to get past this man and the guards. I need to get on that plane.

If the stranger wanted to be reckless, she'd let him trip over his own feet. After all, the man had caused the scene in the first place. But he seemed content to play innocent civilian, which only angered the guard further. A vein jumped on the guard's bright-red neck, making her heart stop. That was enough for Sonny to step in.

"Excuse me. My Spanish is a little rusty," she said. Then she told the guard in Spanish that she was all right and it was all just a misunderstanding.

He seemed to consider her words, then told them to move along or they'd be arrested. She knew that getting arrested would ruin everything for her and the baby.

"My wife and I were just having a little fight. That's all. A disagreement." The stranger didn't appear rattled, but Sonny guessed it was probably an act. How could he not be terrified by staring into the barrel of a gun only a few feet away?

"It's done," she said quietly. "He's letting us go. Thank you," she said to the guard. The less said, the better.

She stared straight ahead and started to walk toward the boarding gate, leaving them all behind. It took considerable strength to keep her breathing easy, as if she had every right to be holding this baby in her arms and taking her through the security gate and out of Colombia for good.

Of course, she did. But if Eduardo Sanchez had anything to say about it, the law in Colombia might not agree with her.

"Sorry to disturb you," she heard the stranger say to the guard. But he came up behind her, taking her arm again and pulling her back. This time the other guard blocked their progress with his gun.

Sonny's heart stopped cold in her chest.

The last call was made for boarding. It was now or never. She needed to be on that plane, not embroiled in a disturbance with the local police. The baby started crying and the loudspeaker drowned out whatever the guard was barking at her. The other guards were watching them with renewed interest.

Digging deep in her soul, she gathered up all her strength. Pasting on a smile, she reached out and kissed the strange man square on the mouth.

Turning back to the guards, she said, "See? It's over. Just a simple lovers' quarrel. You know, *riña?* Sweetheart, our plane is leaving. We need to go."

The stranger's eyes bore into her. With surprise and determination in his voice, he said, "We'll take another flight. I forgot my ticket."

Sonny's stomach churned as she caught the impatient looks from the security crew. She couldn't see the boarding gate beyond security, but she knew the ground crew would only wait so long before they'd close the door without her and she'd miss her chance to get back to the United States—maybe forever.

"I...I'll meet you back home then. I'm sure you can get another ticket. I don't want to miss this flight."

"Look," the man said, bending toward her so only she could hear. "These guards are about as curious as kids on Christmas morning. You give them even the slightest reason to arrest you, they will. If you're lucky. Otherwise, we'll both be going home. In body bags. Again, *if* we're lucky." He smiled tightly as he pulled his head away and looked down at her.

The guard motioned with his gun for them to move

on. She wanted nothing better. But the stranger was pulling her in the opposite direction.

She could make a fuss, but that would only give the guards a reason to detain her, check her papers and maybe confiscate her passport. She and Ellie were going to need them to board the plane in Colombia and get past customs in the U.S.

She couldn't risk it. Word was probably already circulating that the baby was missing. It was only a matter of time before Eduardo Sanchez rallied his men to find her. She couldn't risk the guards looking any closer at Ellie.

"Come on," the stranger said, pulling her away from the boarding gate.

The door leading to the tarmac closed and Sonny's heart sank. She thought of Lucia and all that she gave up to help rescue Ellie. How could she have failed her so miserably? And Ellie's mother, Serena. If Sonny didn't get this baby back to the U.S. safely, how could she ever face her sister-in-law again?

As tears filled her eyes, she glanced in desperation at the people in the terminal and wondered if it would hurt or help to try to get through the door to the tarmac and charge to the plane. She noticed that her little pretense had been enough to satisfy the guard, who had moved on to another group of people trying to get through security with a large bag.

After everything she'd overcome in the past few weeks, the last obstacle was a two-hour flight to Miami and the nightmare would be over.

Through the window, she saw the door to the plane close as a member of the ground crew pulled the mobile stairs away from the plane. Her father would be waiting for them in Miami when that plane landed. So would Tammie, who was Dylan's fiancée and Serena's sister. And so, of course, would Serena. She could only imagine how devastated they would be when she and Ellie didn't get off that plane to greet them.

She only had one choice now. With her resolve set, she turned and faced the stranger.

TWO

"**Y**ou mind telling me just who you are?" Sonny said. Ellie cried out at her harsh tone and she quickly wrapped her arms around the baby to comfort her so she'd quiet down.

The man looked straight at her, his jaw tight and his dark eyes hard. She had the feeling he wasn't in the mood for grilling. Well, that was just fine by her. She wasn't in the mood for him ruining everything she'd worked so hard to accomplish these past weeks.

His eyes scanned the area around them, but he kept still. He was probably checking to make sure the guards had moved on. They had. In a low voice, he said, "I need to talk to you."

"You make me miss my flight and then expect me to talk to you? Forget it! I need to go book another flight." Hopefully she'd be able to get a flight today although the next flight to Miami wasn't until the morning. It didn't even matter where the plane was going as long as it landed somewhere in the United States. Maybe she could cash in her direct flight to Miami for the flight to Houston that she'd seen posted for later in the day. She needed to call her father, but she could do that as soon as she had a ticket in hand.

He chuckled and shook his head, his dark eyes filling with amusement. "Gotta tell you, I didn't expect that kiss but it seemed to do the trick with our trigger boys back there. I thought for sure we were done for and I wasn't relishing the idea of spending the next six months in detainment. What made you think of that?"

"I couldn't help myself. Must be your dazzling charm. You owe me some answers. Who are you and how do you know my brother?"

"Does it really matter?"

Anger surged through her. She tried to rein it in but her voice got louder as she spoke. "You bet it does, bucko. You are responsible for preventing me from bringing my niece back to safety."

"Whoa, whoa. Keep your voice down. I hear you, and whatever you have going on here with the baby doesn't concern me. You just need to tell me where your brother is hiding, and then you can go on your merry way."

She blinked back her surprise. "I don't need to tell you anything. I don't know you." She eyed him suspiciously. "What makes you think I know where Cash is?"

"Why else would a good girl like you be hiding out in Colombia?" He glanced at the baby. "With your *niece*."

He took her arm again, lightly but firmly, as if he didn't want to leave a bruise but still wanted a good grip. Then he started walking her toward the exit. It was then that she noticed two new guards watching them from the front door.

Terrific. That's all she needed. She started walking with him, keeping her eyes straight ahead. When she reached the point where the guards were standing, she gave them a quick smile and continued walking.

Her brain was racing. If she could get away from this man she and Ellie could hide out in the restroom again, or maybe sit in the corner of a restaurant in the terminal. She could find a phone in a quiet place and call the hotel in Miami to warn her father that she hadn't made the flight. Once she was out of sight, she could quickly modify the plans that Lucia made. But reports might be all over the news by then about Eduardo Sanchez's missing "adopted" baby. Maybe there was an earlier flight to the U.S. than the Houston flight. It was risky, but it could be done.

She glanced back through the glass doors. The guards were observing them. Closing her eyes, she muttered a short prayer as she continued to walk. *Lord, you've brought me this far. I know You'll bring us the whole way home.*

Sonny realized that, whether she liked it or not, she was probably going to have to stay the night in Colombia. Her first priority was to get away from this man and the attention he had brought to her. In order to do that, she'd have to leave the airport. The problem was she didn't know her way around Cartagena.

Sonny shook the thought from her head. She couldn't fail. Not just for Cash and baby Ellie. But now for Lucia. She had no choice but to get away from the airport. At least for now.

"Now that you're done hiding, you can give me the information I need," the stranger said, breaking into her thoughts.

"I wasn't hiding. I was on vacation," Sonny said. "You know, people *do* have vacations."

"Sure they do. You were on vacation," he said sarcastically. "And my name is Alice and I live in a place called Wonderland."

"I guess I can call you Al, then?"

He threw her a wry grin and pushed the door open. Sonny scanned the parking lot to see if anyone was paying attention to them.

"Come with me. I have a ride waiting for us."

Sonny knew that the last thing she needed was to have to flag down a taxi. She'd heard that taxi drivers in Cartagena happily snowed you if you didn't know the city. However, it was still safer to take a taxi than walk anywhere. American tourists with American dollars were targets for criminals.

The fact that she was still on airport grounds put both Ellie and her at risk. But could she really take a chance on this guy and his ride, whoever that was?

Another problem dawned on her as the sun beat down on her head. She was almost out of money. She'd paid for the hotel room and her meals with cash. Colombians liked U.S. dollars and there were enough tourists down here that American cash couldn't be traced back to her. But she'd stayed longer than she'd expected and had gone through her reserve. She had a credit card, but credit cards were way too traceable, and she knew she needed to be careful.

Careful? Yeah, right. They'd done everything as planned and Lucia was still dead. Except for the fact that this little baby who was now crying loud enough to drown out the street noise was finally in her arms, it had all gone wrong.

Sonny wanted to cry, too, but she bit back the tears. There'd be time for that later. It wouldn't do either of them any good if she broke down now. It certainly wouldn't get her on that plane that was taxiing down the runway on its way to Miami.

"Oh, Lucia," she whispered, closing her eyes. "I promise I won't let you down."

"What was that?"

They were still standing on the curb and for a moment, Sonny had forgotten someone was with her.

She pushed away thoughts of Lucia and fought for composure. "Who are you and how do you know my brother?" she asked again.

He put his fingers in his mouth and whistled. Sonny tried to cover Ellie's ears, but the baby was flailing as she cried.

"I don't think anyone is going to appreciate your breaking their eardrums."

"It's hot and we're sitting ducks here. It's time to go."

A car rolled to a stop in front of them. The man stepped off the curb and opened the back door, gesturing for her to get inside.

"This is our ride. Get in."

She shot him a disbelieving look. "Are you out of your mind? What makes you think I'm going to get into a car with you before I even know who you are?" Sonny asked, knowing full well that she had no other option.

"Gillespie Waite. You can call me Gil."

"That's it?"

"I introduced myself."

"I'm not getting in that car until you tell me what I want to know. People have a bad habit of disappearing in this country and this baby and I are not going to end up on that list."

He stared at her, considering what she'd said. "You don't have to be afraid. I'm not here to hurt you."

He smiled and for a fraction of a second, he didn't look as suspicious as he had in the airport.

"And?" she pressed.

"I was hired to find your brother. Cash Montgomery is your brother, isn't he? He was arrested in Chicago on drug trafficking charges and then fled before his hearing."

"Says you. My family and I know he was framed. Who hired you?"

"His bail bondsman. You can take up the 'framed' theory with him and the federal prosecutor."

"What's the bail bondsman's name?" Sonny couldn't remember the name offhand but she was sure she'd recognize it if he told her. She wanted to know if Gil really knew it or if he was just giving her a line to shut her up.

"Does it matter?"

"To me it does. You've just ruined my chance of getting this baby out of Colombia safely."

"You said that before." He leaned forward and whispered in her ear, "I wouldn't go yelling that too loudly. Especially since something tells me you're not exactly running with the law yourself right now."

She stifled her defeated sigh. "The name?"

"Telling you the name of the bondsman isn't going to change the fact that you and the kid need to get into the car before we draw any more attention to ourselves than we already have. As I've told you, these guards are trigger-happy. We may have fooled them inside the airport, but we won't get lucky like that twice."

"You call me missing my plane lucky?"

He continued, his voice booming over hers. "All they

need is just a hint of a reason to put some pressure on that trigger and let those bullets spray. It doesn't even need to be a good reason. And they don't care how much of a mess they make. Get my drift? 'Cause they're not going to do the cleaning up."

She did know. She knew what kind of people her family was dealing with. It pained her to think that Cash had fallen into the hands of men who were so willing to do him harm, the likes of which had already been done to Lucia.

Gil held the door to the backseat open. Sonny fixed her eyes on him, taking in the hard look of challenge on his face. She was up to that challenge, but how could she drag Ellie into it? If she screamed, the authorities would come running and she had no doubt it would end in bloodshed, just like Gil said. Every instinct she had told her it was a bad idea to go with this man. Isn't that what self-defense classes taught women? You're as good as dead if you get into the car?

But he knew about Cash. And in her arms was Cash's little daughter, a baby that Lucia had just given her life to free—despite what Torres had said, she knew Lucia's death was because of Ellie. She had no idea where Dylan was or if he was any closer to locating Cash. In a way, Gil was all she had.

And dead was dead, whether by his hand or the guards who had their own brand of justice. She could only hope he'd have mercy on the baby. "What's in this for you?" she said, trying one last time for information.

"I take your brother back to the U.S. for prosecution before the bail needs to be paid and I get a nice bonus for my troubles. That's the way it works."

"Do you take us, too?"

The words were out of her mouth before she had time to think about what she'd said. The surprise in his eyes mirrored what she felt. But it was the only way. She'd come far, but she couldn't do this alone. She needed help and if she worked this right, she and Ellie might be able to get back to the States alive.

"Look, you're the one who is responsible for me missing my plane. I don't have any more money to pay for food or hotel rooms. If you're going to detain me until you get whatever information you think I have—"

"Go on. Get in," he said quietly.

She closed her eyes and sighed softly. Ellie was still fussing, though much more quietly than before. She needed a diaper change and a bottle, neither of which she'd get while Sonny stood there and debated.

Gil was after money. She was out of it. He wanted her brother. She wanted safety for all of them. If Gil could find Cash, that was just an added bonus, wasn't it? With her plane long gone and the airport guards suspicious of her, she had only one choice. She had to go with him.

She stepped off the curb and into the backseat, hoping she hadn't just made the worst mistake of her life.

They'd ditched the other car twenty minutes ago for a nondescript tourist vehicle that blended in with all the other rentals on the road. It didn't have that new-car smell that cars in the U.S. had. This one had been used. A lot. It was an older model that would have been traded in years ago and sold on a used car lot back in the States.

Sonny wasn't complaining—it had provided a place for her to change Ellie's diaper and put a bottle together to feed her.

Gil didn't say anything about where they were going and Sonny didn't ask. She was emotionally spent, relishing the quiet and grateful for the opportunity it gave her to say a silent prayer to the Lord. He'd brought her this far. Much farther than she'd thought was possible. The fact that she was now holding her brother's daughter in her arms was proof of His grace. That alone held her disappointment and frustration at bay.

If Dylan knew what was going on, he'd have a cow— Sonny was sure of it. Both Tammie and Serena had wanted to make the trip, but it was too dangerous for them. The very people who'd kidnapped Ellie were still out for vengeance on their family and would recognize Serena and Tammie immediately, especially since they looked almost identical.

The car turned down a side street. Sonny braced one arm on the seat in front of her to stay upright with the baby in her other arm. No car seat. She lost good-aunt points on that note. But she hadn't expected to be in a car with Ellie again.

They hit a deep pothole in the middle of the street. Sonny gasped as her head nearly hit the roof of the car. Gil turned back to her.

"You two okay?" he asked.

Sonny took a moment to study his face. He was a bit older than she was, by about five or six years, making him Cash's age. He had a slight build with broad shoulders that almost didn't fit his frame. His hair was dark, thick and wavy, and his eyes were so brown they were almost black. Could they be that dark? She wondered. Maybe it was just the lack of light on this sheltered side street that made them seem that way.

There was a hard gruffness about Gil, yet when he glanced at the baby, Sonny could swear she saw a faint smile, as if the big bad wolf was showing a soft side.

Sonny was about to reply when the female driver, who Gil had referred to as Cooper, spoke.

"Marco is still trying to hack into that Web site," she said.

"Any luck?"

"Nada."

Gil grimaced and shook his head. "This is not good. We need more."

Cooper gestured to the backseat. "Did she tell you anything?"

"Only that she doesn't know where Cash is but she wants to find him, too."

"She speaks fluent Spanish?" Cooper asked.

"She seems to."

"She's in the car, by the way," Sonny called out from the backseat, sounding as annoyed as she felt. "She has a name and she wants to know where we are going."

"Sorry. We're headed to a hotel on the coast with some small villas in the old part of Cartagena. We have to make sure we look like we're tourists," Gil said.

Cooper added, "When we get there, you can tell us all about your brother."

Sonny stared at the eyes that met her in the rear-view mirror. "What makes you think I'm going to tell you anything?"

"Because believe it or not, we want to find your

brother alive as much as you do," Cooper said sarcastically.

Sonny turned to Gil. "Who's this?"

The driver glared at Sonny in the rearview mirror.

"Calm down, Cooper." Gil chuckled and shook his head. "Cooper's a member of my team, Miss Montgomery. She's not all that fond of Colombia, either. It's making her cranky. Although it could be that she's been spending a little too much time with me and Marco. We might be rubbing off on her."

"Knock it off, *Gillespie*," Cooper snapped. "Excuse me if I'm a little tired of waiting around in the hotel all day while you sightsee and Marco plays on the computer."

Gil pretended to be hurt. "Ouch. And I doubt Marco will be happy to hear you said that."

With a roll of her eyes, Cooper added, "I'm scared."

Gil laughed.

It was obvious the two had worked together for a while and felt comfortable sparring. Sonny watched Cooper in the mirror. She wasn't exactly a pretty woman, but whatever attractive features she had were eclipsed by the fact that she did nothing to make herself look more feminine. Her hair was cut short to her scalp and she wore no makeup or jewelry.

Sonny pulled her gaze to the scenery. When had she become so vain? She was used to dressing on the more casual side, preferring an old pair of jeans that were worn and patched in spots to pants or skirts. Sneakers won over shoes—never mind heels—most days of the week. Cooper was different, though, as if she was trying to conceal the fact that she was a woman. Maybe in her line of work she had to.

"We'll see what we can get out of her when we get back," Gil finally said.

"What are you going to do?" Sonny chimed in, tired of their rudeness. "Beat it out of me?"

Cooper rolled her eyes in the rearview mirror and then settled them back on the road.

Gil turned to her. "Don't be ridiculous."

"Everything about this is ridiculous. Why shouldn't I be, too?"

He turned around and they were all quiet for a while. Sonny used that time to hold the baby close. She hadn't allowed herself the luxury of really looking at Ellie, of enjoying her like she would if they'd been somewhere safe. In the airport bathroom, she'd been afraid someone would see her and know right away that Sonny was not Ellie's mother.

But now she studied the warm baby in her arms. Ellie looked a little like Cash, but mostly she looked like Sonny's mother.

She wondered what her mother was thinking right now. She must be worried. She'd had a lot to worry about recently with all that had happened with Cash. Finding out that Cash had secretly married Serena and that they'd had a child who'd been kidnapped had been quite a shock for all of them. But Sonny knew her mother wanted her granddaughter home as much as the rest of the family did, and that she'd put aside any fears she had about Sonny coming to Colombia.

Ellie had settled now that she'd had her bottle. Sonny knew next to nothing about taking care of babies. But she knew her brother Cash didn't, either, and he'd entered the world of parenthood. She was a quick learner and she'd do anything she could to keep Ellie safe, happy and healthy. Anything.

"Tell me again where we're going?" she said, breaking the silence.

Gil glanced back at her, giving the baby a quick look. "Somewhere a little more comfortable than that dive you holed up in these last few weeks."

Her eyes widened. "You were watching me?"

His smile was quick. "Don't be so surprised. My talents are many." When she didn't appear amused, his smile faded. "It's my job. It's what I do."

Gil had been watching her. This man that she'd only laid eyes on a few short hours ago had been watching her and she'd never even suspected. She closed her eyes as disappointment washed over her. No wonder something had gone wrong. Had her carelessness given Lucia away, too?

She tried to push the thoughts invading her mind aside. For now, anyway. There'd be time enough later to sort through what had happened and what had gone wrong. Right now, she had to concentrate on what to do next.

"Don't worry. You'll both be safe from whatever you're running from where we're going."

Tears filled her eyes, blurring her vision. He said the words as if he actually believed them. What a nice feeling that must be.

"There isn't such a place," she answered. "At least, not here in Colombia."

Maybe nowhere in the world.

THREE

The woman was an enigma, Gil thought as he turned his attention back to the road, which was still slick from a hard rain the night before. He'd prepared himself for more rain today. In fact, he would have preferred torrential rain for the rest of the long ride from the airport to the villa instead of a brightly shining sun. It would drown out this nagging doubt that coursed through his veins.

He'd expected Sonny Montgomery to give him a bit more of a fight. Thinking of the baby in her arms, he wasn't sure how much of a fight she actually could have put up. Ellie was the reason she'd given in so readily. She'd really had no other option than to go with him.

Well, no matter. They were already skating pretty close to the legal line in the first place by picking her up at the airport. If Sonny wanted to leave once they got to the villa, there wasn't anything the team could do to stop her—she wasn't the criminal. But if they could do a little good-cop-bad-cop routine before she left, she might spill her brother's whereabouts and they could all go home a little sooner.

They drove in relative quiet, except for the occasional whimper from the baby as she stirred in her sleep. They followed the highway until it spilled them into the coastal city of Cartagena where tourists were milling about in shorts, sandals and straw hats they probably paid too much for from street vendors who had a hard time taking no for an answer. The team had an easier time blending in here than back in Monteria or at the airport where soldiers seemed to outnumber civilians.

A bead of sweat journeyed its way down the side of Gil's neck. The coast should be a bit cooler, what with the sea breeze and the air-conditioning in the villa.

His boss's expense account was paying for their digs as long as they didn't overstay their usefulness in Colombia. Jared was good that way, but only if it produced results.

It was a pretty place, Gil thought as the car pulled into the parking lot of the main villa. Marco had already checked in, but was only able to acquire one key. They'd need at least two.

"How are we traveling this time?" he asked Cooper.

"Married couples," she said, cutting the engine and pocketing the keys. "Marco and I checked out of the singles at the other hotel before sunrise this morning and camped out at the office until it opened. We got a two-bedroom suite. He's been setting up his equipment all day, trying to get connected, but Internet access is spotty down here."

Gil blew out a breath. He figured as much. "Okay, we'll take what we can get then, I guess."

Married couples. Gil almost laughed. He couldn't think of himself that way. He'd been part of a couple only a few times in his thirty-three years. Once, he'd almost landed at the altar, but luckily they'd both done a little soul-searching and decided it wasn't what either of them really wanted.

Cooper jumped out of the car and made her way to the front office. In the three years he'd known her, he'd never seen her wear a dress or even shorts. He couldn't even say if she really had legs underneath the baggy pants she always wore.

Marco had teased her once about her clothes only to be on the receiving end of a few pointed words. Rumor had it she'd been roughed up by a gang of hoods in college on her way back to the dormitory one night. Since then, she just found it easier to downplay whatever feminine assets she had.

As she climbed the stairs two at a time in her clunky boots, Gil figured she was playing it as close to the ground as she could get. It was one way to survive. Couldn't fault her for that.

"You have no idea what you've done by taking me here," Sonny said from the backseat, sounding tired. "My brother Dylan is a Chicago police officer." She paused. "But then you must know all about Dylan, too, I suppose."

"That's right," he said, finally looking at her. "Why don't you just keep yourself comfortable until we get into the villa? Then you can tell me all about what I don't know."

The minutes stretched on unbearably and Gil was thankful when Cooper appeared, running back to the car. It gave him an excuse to stop looking at Sonny in the rearview mirror and taking note of her sad, ocean-blue eyes.

Coward, he chided himself. The way she sat there,

holding the baby as if he'd snatch her away at any moment, showed how terrified she was. He didn't like scaring her like that but it was necessary if he was going to get any information about Cash.

"All set?"

Cooper nodded and gunned the engine.

In under a minute, they pulled up next to Marco's car in front of a small villa. Gil got out of the front seat quickly, glad not to be cooped up in such cramped quarters after the long ride.

So close to the equator, the temperatures held steady all year round at about eighty degrees. The back of Gil's shirt was sticky with sweat and he was looking forward to a little AC to help cool off.

As he opened the passenger door and stepped out, he could smell the warm Caribbean Sea only a few blocks away.

"Nice place Jared set us up with," he called out to Cooper. Then he turned his attention to Sonny in the backseat. He opened the back door, but she just sat there holding the baby.

"What's wrong?"

Sonny glared up at him. "You really have to ask?"

"I'm not taking you to your death."

"How do I know that?"

Gil was taken aback. Did she really think he was going to hurt her?

"I told you who we are. I haven't kidnapped you, Sonny."

It was important to make that clear to her. Although he'd basically given her no choice back at the airport, she *was* free to leave at any time. Of course, they could tail her and make her life miserable until they got what they wanted. But that wasn't illegal—especially in Colombia.

"Then why didn't you let me get on that plane? I could have been in Miami by now."

"I told you. I need your help to find your brother. As soon as we find him, you can get on a flight to Miami."

"You can't find him, so you figure I'll just bring you to him, right? Well, I hate to disappoint you, Mr. Waite, but I haven't seen or heard from my brother in more than four months. If you want to find him, you'll have to ask the people who framed him on those bogus drug trafficking charges. Because I have no idea where he is. But rest assured that even if I did, I wouldn't help you chase him down. Cash is an innocent man."

The baby was crying again. Sonny fought hard not to break down herself. She longed for the comfort of a familiar voice, to lay her head down on her pillow and sleep without worry. No dreams. No nightmares. No waking with awful visions of things that could—and did—go wrong. Just pure blissful sleep.

Since Cash had gone missing, her imagination had gone wild. Fear stabbed her heart as she pictured what her father was probably going through now that the plane had landed in Miami without her and the baby.

She had to figure out how to get word to him. Somehow.

The day had gone wretchedly wrong and now she had a bounty hunter staring her down, wanting her to get out of the car. But as she looked up at him, his expression had changed from impatience to interest.

"He was framed on bogus drug trafficking charges, huh? Why don't you come inside and tell me all about it. It's a lot better than sitting out here in the heat. And you can tend to the baby much easier in the villa."

"You mean out of earshot? Where no one will realize that I'm being held against my will?"

"I told you—"

"Yeah, yeah, I know. I can leave if I want. But what choice do I really have? You'd just follow me again. Keep me from getting on another plane."

"Come inside and we'll talk about your choices." His voice was low and held a trace of sympathy. She wasn't sure if she should use that to her advantage now, or wait until a better opportunity presented itself.

"I need more diapers. I only had enough to get me back to the States."

Gil nodded. "I'll send Cooper out to get whatever you need."

It would have to do. It'd been risky enough for her to be in Monteria *without* the baby, but being in Cartagena *with* the baby was even more dangerous now that news reports were probably flooding the local TV station about Eduardo Sanchez's missing baby. She needed to stay out of sight.

She resigned herself to going inside with Gil. He helped her out of the car, and they stepped through the door into the foyer of the beautiful villa. She would have enjoyed staying here under different circumstances, but as the door closed behind her, she could practically hear iron bars locking into place.

"Shh," she cooed to the fussing baby, hoping to soothe her. She doubted she could. In her niece's short life, she had been kept a secret, kidnapped and trans-ported to a South American country and rescued by a woman she didn't know at all. The fact that they were related meant nothing to the baby, and Sonny's attempts to comfort were feeble at best. But she vowed to build a strong relationship with her niece. Hopefully in the United States, surrounded by their family.

The cool air inside bathed her face—it was a welcome relief from the hot car. One look at Gil and she knew he was probably thinking the same thing. He grabbed a can of soda from the refrigerator and rolled it across his forehead before cracking it open and taking a long gulp.

"Help yourself," he said, taking another sip. "There's plenty. I don't think there's any milk for the baby, though."

"She doesn't drink milk yet. Just formula." Suddenly an awful thought struck her. "Cooper and Marco didn't use my name, did they? When they checked us in?" she added quickly. Her heart pounded like a timpani in her chest. If anyone knew she was here…

With the can still poised in the air, Gil stared at her quizzically. "Why?"

"Did they?" she pressed.

A man she hadn't met yet, presumably Marco, came into the room. "We used 'Mr. and Mrs.,'" he said. "My name and Gil's. Makes it simple."

Her relief was obvious.

Gil was standing in front of her now. "Why?"

She looked up at his dark eyes. Yes, they were as dark as they'd appeared in the car. It hadn't been the light. She drew in a deep breath. "I need to get the baby settled."

"I told you. Cooper can take care—"

"Cooper isn't Ellie's aunt." She hadn't intended her voice to be so harsh. Gil looked as surprised as she felt at her outburst, but she didn't care. She was entitled to be sharp with him—what she'd gone through today was nothing short of a nightmare. Lucia, an innocent woman who'd vowed to help, was dead. And it was Sonny's fault. The reason Lucia had put her life in danger was because Sonny had asked her to.

"You mentioned the baby was your niece."

She closed her eyes. "Yes."

Gil looked down at the baby. "Cash's?"

The way he was probing, they'd find out soon enough. She nodded.

Gil glanced at Marco. "Did you know about this?"

Marco shook his head. "Nothing about a baby came up in my research." He was rummaging through paperwork on his makeshift desk at the table. "No wife. Not even a girlfriend as far as I could tell."

They were all looking at her now, questions silently blasting at her from their accusing stares.

"Why isn't there a record of this baby?"

Sonny couldn't help the smug grin that sprang to her face. "I thought you knew everything."

"I know Cash Montgomery is a drug dealer and he jumped bail. That's all I need to know."

Irritation coiled inside her. "If that's the case, then you don't need me at all. If you'll show me my room, I'd like to make a list for Cooper and then give the baby a bath."

She turned to leave, but Cooper caught her arm. "How is it that you came down to Colombia alone and now you have your brother's baby in tow?" At a glance from Gil, Cooper released her. "If something is going on, if you're afraid, we can help," she said, more gently.

"Help who? Is that what you think you're doing? You people truly have no idea what you've done today," she said, repeating what she'd already said to Gil for Marco's and Cooper's benefit. "None at all."

"How'd you get the baby, Sonny? You need to come clean and tell us," Cooper said.

"Not now. Ellie needs me."

There were two beds in the room they'd given Sonny. Both were big and covered with soft pillows and bedding. After her outburst in the living room, she was totally drained. But she couldn't sleep until she tended to the baby. And she wasn't ready to let her guard down, anyway. She still had no idea if she could trust these people.

Ellie's last bottle was long gone, drained in the car on the drive to the villa. She didn't need to feel the heaviness of the baby's diaper to know she needed a change. The scent was enough to let her know.

Pushing the pillows aside and placing a towel on the bed, she lay the sleeping baby down and began to undress her, hoping she could change the diaper without waking her. As she searched her bag for a clean diaper, tears welled up in her eyes and began to fall.

She was still in Colombia. She'd failed, and Lucia was dead. How was she going to explain this to her father? That is, if she even had the chance to talk to him. Somehow she had to get word to him.

Right about now, Dylan was risking his life to get to Cash. Somehow. She didn't know the details. They'd all agreed Sonny was better off not knowing so they could each focus on their specific mission. But the truth was that they didn't want her to know any details in case she got caught.

Well, she'd been caught, in a manner of speaking. By the grace of God, Cash would make it safely home, but what about her and Ellie?

Dear Lord, help me get my niece back to safety. I know I've been asking for a lot these days but...

She wiped a tear off her cheek with the back of her hand. She knew without a doubt that if it was God's will, she'd make it home. Dylan had always said that some burdens were heavier to bear than others. The Lord wouldn't give her anything more than she could handle. He also told her that whenever she felt she couldn't go on, she should do what she could and offer the rest up to God.

Well, there was a whole lot she couldn't handle these days but it didn't seem right not to do her part when so many others were putting their lives on the line, too. She took a moment and said a prayer to the Lord to give her strength, to help her be strong enough to see this through. And she offered up to Him what she couldn't control.

She turned at a knock on the door. Cooper walked in.

"Nice digs, huh?" she said with a smile. It was the first time Cooper had smiled since they'd met.

"Do you have that list that Gil asked you to write up?"

Sonny closed the last tab on the diaper and carefully placed Ellie in the middle of the bed. "Just give me a second."

She washed her hands and then grabbed the pad of

paper that was sitting between the beds. Ellie was awake now and looking around at the strange surroundings, stretching and turning to see who was in the room with her. Within seconds she rolled over onto her stomach.

Sonny sat on the bed beside her, a pang of fear hitting her square in the chest. She'd left the baby alone in the middle of the bed when she could have easily rolled off. She didn't know all that much about babies, being the youngest in her family, but clearly Ellie was old enough to turn over on her own now. She'd have to remember that.

She quickly scratched down the essentials and decided that would probably be enough for now. If need be, she could send someone out again. Maybe by then she'd have a plan to get out of this mess.

Folding the slip of paper, she handed it to Cooper. "I don't know your first name."

The other woman finally met her eyes. "Brooke."

Sonny nodded. "That's a pretty name."

"Thanks."

"Why don't they ever call you that?"

As she got a good look at Cooper, she felt bad that she'd thought of her as masculine. There was nothing masculine about her except for her short hair. She had pretty eyes and a small, upturned nose.

"I like to keep gender out of things. It's easier that way." She headed for the door and then turned. "I'll be right back. You look a little tired. You might want to get some rest. You're in for a long day."

The door closed and for a moment, Sonny felt like a prisoner. There were no bars on the windows or chains on her hands and feet. But the feeling that she was all alone, confined to a cell, consumed her.

As tired as she was, she wasn't about to stay cooped up. She scooped Ellie in her arms, cooing until the baby's face lit with a smile. That smile alone was worth all the fear and frustration and exhaustion she'd been feeling.

As she walked into the common area, she saw Gil slumped on a cushy floral sofa, his feet propped up on the coffee table. He straightened up as she approached.

"I thought you'd be taking a nap," he said.

"Can't sleep. The baby slept most of the way and now she's awake. I don't have a crib to put her in and I don't want her to roll off the bed and get hurt."

He nodded. "I'll call the main desk to see if they have a portable crib. This hotel caters to tourists so we might be in luck. Are you hungry? The villa has a small kitchen and Marco stocked up on food earlier."

She was about to say no when Marco came barreling in from the kitchen holding a piece of paper. "Aztec Corporation deals with shipping art and artifacts. Big deal. Everyone ships something or other down here." He stopped short when he saw Sonny standing there.

Sonny felt the blood drain from her face. "And how did you find out about Aztec Corporation?"

"Marco's a research genius," Gil said, looking at her closely. "He did some digging around in your brother's records and it seems he had some connection to the Aztec Corporation. Mind filling us in?"

"I can't, sorry," she said, trying to stay calm.

Marco shrugged. "I'll keep looking," he said to Gil. "Unfortunately, the kitchen's the only place we can get an Internet connection. Sometimes. It keeps cutting out on me."

Her pulse quickened. *They had a computer.* She remembered Cooper and Gil talking about Marco hacking into a file. They must have been trying to hack into the Aztec Corporation Web site she'd found before coming to Colombia. That was how she'd found Ellie. Like Marco, Sonny was good with computers. More than good.

She'd have to be careful. She was sure Gil and his team knew full well what she did for a living.

Sonny feigned disinterest. "Gil said you went on a food run earlier? I'm starving," she said, creating a good reason to check out their setup in the kitchen.

"There's not much." He looked almost apologetic as he gestured at Ellie. "I didn't know there'd be a baby here."

"Do you have any fruit? I could probably cut up something for her."

"There are some bananas."

Sonny nodded. "Great. She might like that."

"Wait, don't you have to be careful what you give babies at this age?" Marco said, worry lines creasing his brow.

Gil laughed. "How would you know?"

Marco lifted his hands in protest. "I don't. But my sister always said that about my nephew. He had food allergies."

Sonny hadn't thought of that. She felt way out of her depth. But how much harm could bananas do?

"Maybe we could look up what babies eat at this age. Online, I mean," she said, realizing that was a perfect opportunity.

"Sure. Better to be safe than have the kid break out in red spots or something."

"They do that?" Gil asked, grimacing.

"Yeah, my nephew swelled up with hives all over his body. Totally disgusting. It freaked me out."

"Why don't you check the kitchen for something that won't make Ellie swell up with hives all over the place," Gil said with a chuckle. "I don't want to see Marco freak out."

She smiled and went to the kitchen with Marco on her heels. The computer was on the counter near the telephone. It was hard not to run over and start using it. Instead, she looked at the food that was spread out on the counter.

"Find anything?" Gil said, standing in the doorway.

"I'm not sure. This vanilla pudding might be too sweet for her."

"Applesauce," Marco said, reaching past her. "They didn't have those little snack packs but I did find a small jar. My sister always gave my nephew applesauce."

She smiled at him in thanks but out of the corner of her eye, she saw the computer, practically calling to her. Marco had set up an office in the kitchen. Her mind was racing. She could contact her father, tell him what had happened.

"Did you call about the crib?" she asked Gil.

His eyes met hers and held for a brief moment. Sonny was tempted to pull away from his gaze but she fought to hold the stare. She didn't want him or anyone else intimidating her. But the look he gave her was not one of intimidation. It was of sympathy and it almost made her crumble.

"They said someone would bring it up later," he said quietly.

"I'm really tired," she said, shifting the baby in her arms with exaggerated fatigue. "If you don't mind, can you two go down to the office and see if you can carry it back here? After I feed the baby, I'm going to try to nap. I'll feel more comfortable if Ellie is in a crib."

"Sure," he said. "Let's go, Marco."

Nothing about this job felt right, Gil thought. He rubbed his hand over his head as he and Marco struggled with the crib through the parking lot.

"You didn't come up with anything on a wife?" Gil asked.

"Nothing," Marco said.

"Terrific." This was going to complicate things. In the past hour since they'd made it back to the villa, he'd begun to believe that Sonny Montgomery really didn't know where Cash was hiding out. A baby and the possibility of a wife changed things. If they'd known, they'd have tailed the wife, tried to appeal to her concern for her husband's safety.

"What about Aztec?" he said. They'd hit a dead end and needed a break. The Aztec Corporation could be the very thing that broke this case wide-open.

"I can't tell if they're legit. All these shipping companies look fine on the surface. I have to dig into their private files to see what they're all about." Marco's eyes lit up. He loved a good excuse to hack deep. "What do you say, boss man? Want to go on a hunt?"

Gil laughed, rolling his eyes. "I'll leave that one up to you. See how easy it is to break into their sys—"

He stopped short, pulling Marco back as they reached the villa.

"Did you leave your computer on in the kitchen?" Gil asked.

"No, I shut it down. Don't worry, it's password protected."

Gil thought a second. "She's a hacker by trade, Marco."

Marco looked at the crib in his hands. "You think she snowed us?"

"We'll find out in a minute. Hang here for a second," he said, and moved past Marco into the villa, leaving the door ajar.

He moved quietly, looking toward the bedrooms and around the living room. Sonny had said she was going to feed the baby and then take a nap. She was probably still feeding Ellie—he could hear the baby making noise in the kitchen.

As he moved toward the kitchen, he heard a distinctive sound that was *not* a spoon going into a baby's mouth.

"You type pretty fast with a baby in your arms," he said, leaning against the doorjamb.

Sonny quickly punched a key and the screen went blank. She straightened up and turned to Gil.

He'd felt sorry for her, with everything she'd been dealing with. But here she was, having tricked them into giving her computer access. She was warning her brother. Gil was sure of it.

"Maybe we'll hold off on the nap so we can have a good chat," he said, his voice icy. He hated being duped and Sonny had just duped him big-time. Her whole routine had been an act. "You're a criminal just like your brother, aren't you, Ms. Montgomery?"

FOUR

She'd expected them to come back to the villa quickly. But she hadn't gauged the time it would take her to get into the password-protected computer with one hand while holding Ellie with the other.

"I beg your pardon?" Sonny said, answering Gil's accusing stare.

"We brought the crib. That is, if you still need it."

"Why wouldn't I need a crib?"

"I don't know. Wasn't the crib just a ploy to get me and Marco out of the villa so you could go online?"

Sonny glared at him. "You're absolutely right," she said. "That was just one part of my master plan. The first step was to lure you into bringing me back to this villa so I wouldn't have to get on that plane to Miami. How did you know?"

"Don't play with me," he said.

"I have no intention of doing that."

"What *are* you doing?"

She shifted her weight and propped the baby on her hip. Ellie wasn't heavy, but Sonny's arms weren't used to holding a baby this long, especially while multi-tasking. "For your information, I was seeing if I could get an Internet connection to search for safe foods for the baby. After what Marco said about hives, I got worried."

He considered what she said. "Someone left their baby in your care and you know nothing about babies?"

She softened—and almost laughed—because she'd actually been thinking the same thing. She was a pitiful caregiver for Ellie. But that would change soon. She'd learn fast.

"This trip was a way for me to get to know my niece. I'm the youngest in my family and I've never really been around babies before."

"Did you find what you were looking for?"

She shook her head. "The connection kept going out."

"Yo, Gil!" Marco called from the front door of the villa. "Mind giving me a hand here?"

"Be right there," he called out. Then he turned to Sonny. "How old is she?"

"Five months."

"Some doctors don't start babies on solid food until they're a little bit older."

She cocked her head to one side. "Can I trust that information comes from experience?"

He didn't answer. Instead, he looked around the small kitchen and picked up a banana. "I'll have Cooper go out tomorrow for some baby food. In the meantime, you should mash up a banana."

She felt her brow crease. "Is that really necessary?"

His eyebrows raised. "Mashing could help you take out some of your aggression toward me. We may not have enough bananas to satisfy that, though."

She rolled her eyes at his attempt at humor. "I have no desire to take my aggressions out on innocent bananas. What I meant to say is, are we really going to be here so long that I'll need more supplies than what Cooper gets today?"

The glint in his eyes showed amusement. "You're already unhappy with the accommodations? I can call management to see if they have better digs."

"Don't get funny with me," she said, ignoring the sudden feeling she got from looking into his dark eyes. "I want to go back home. I just want to know how long it'll be before we can return to the United States."

He hesitated and put the banana he'd been holding back on the counter with the others. "I'm not leaving Colombia without your brother. So if you're planning on leaving when I do, you can expect to stay as long as it takes to find him."

"Gil! Have a heart. It's hot out here," Marco yelled impatiently.

She closed her eyes as he turned away. "Then we may be waiting a long time," she muttered.

Sonny had uttered her words quietly. However, Gil abruptly turned back and stared at her. His dark eyes didn't look as ferocious as they had when he'd walked into the kitchen a few minutes ago. They'd softened some and Sonny found she actually liked looking at them.

"Is there something you want to tell me, Sonny?"

She thought about it a moment. She'd already told Gil she didn't know where her brother was and it was clear he didn't believe her. Could she trust him enough to tell him the truth about Ellie?

At this point, no matter how much of a mess he'd made for her back at the airport, she had to trust that he'd keep her and Ellie safe. She had no choice. Stepping outside the walls of the villa would only open them up to trouble if Eduardo Sanchez and his people were to discover she and Ellie were here.

She shifted the baby in her arms. Ellie had one hand tangled in the hair that had fallen from Sonny's ponytail, and was reaching for Sonny's earring with the other.

Gently easing her hair out of the baby's grip, she said, "I have to feed the baby."

Disappointment clouded those dark eyes she couldn't seem to stop looking into. Gil left the room without another word and suddenly the small kitchen felt empty.

"You think she's sending us on a wild-goose chase?" Cooper asked, straddling the backward chair with her elbow propped up on top of it and her chin resting on her palm.

Gil sighed and took a swig of cola. "Who knows?" When he'd caught Sonny on the computer earlier, he was sure she'd been trying to contact her brother. And it made him angry.

He should let it go—it wasn't like she was the first person to lie to him. Family members of fugitives were a funny bunch. They wanted to help their loved ones, but they always seemed to do it the wrong way and get themselves in trouble. He'd hate to see that happen with Sonny.

"Don't sweat it. It's not the first time you two have been conned by a pretty girl."

Cooper laughed at the face Gil made, but it grated

on him that maybe there was more than a little truth to her statement. At least this time. He'd always been careful to separate his job from his personal life. But he couldn't deny that he found Sonny Montgomery attractive. Okay, more than that. Something about her kept her on his mind, even when she wasn't in the room.

He turned away from Cooper's snickering and looked into the kitchen where Marco was perched on a stool, working furiously on the computer. "There may not be anything to find, Marco."

"I'm already halfway there," Marco said, spinning in his chair to face Gil. "If she e-mailed Montgomery, we'll find out."

With any luck, by nightfall they'd have an idea of how to find Cash.

Getting up from the sofa, Gil made his way into the kitchen to pour himself a cup of coffee. The first sip told him the coffee had been sitting a while—it was like sludge going down his throat.

He blinked to get some moisture in his dry eyes. The day was crashing down on him. It wouldn't be long before he'd need some serious rest, but he'd have to wait until he had a chance to talk to Sonny again.

She'd holed up in the bedroom since their interaction in the kitchen. He hadn't meant to jump on her. She'd looked terrified when she'd turned around and seen him standing at the kitchen door. Yet she didn't back down. She just lifted her chin and said her piece as if she had every right to use the computer.

He'd almost congratulated her—she had chops, that's for sure. But then he'd reminded himself why he was in Colombia in the first place.

Walking through the living room to the far corner, he pushed open the French doors that led to a small private courtyard. Although the villa was big, he needed some space. Some space away from Sonny Montgomery.

Stepping outside, Gil found the night air was warm and didn't cool him off the way he'd hoped it would. With coffee cup in hand, he sat down on a bench in the center of the courtyard next to some potted plants. The moon was bright. Not quite full, but getting there. A chaise lounge would be nice, he thought. He could sleep under the stars like he used to in the military. He'd always liked nights like that. They brought clarity even if they didn't bring answers.

Back then it was a time to pray. He'd talk to the Lord like He was sitting right there. Funny how he'd never seemed to do that during the day, and now, not at all. The black sky had always seemed like a comforting blanket that protected him when he needed to find solace in his faith. He had a hard time feeling that same sense of comfort now. He was on edge—and part of him knew that was because of their houseguest.

Something about the way Sonny had looked at him when they'd first arrived at the villa didn't sit right with him. He prided himself on the job he did nabbing criminals who deserved to be brought to justice. But Sonny had looked at him as if he might really hurt her and the baby. She *believed* that he could. And that bothered him more than he wanted to admit.

He shook it off. It didn't really matter what Sonny Montgomery thought about him or his job. His boss was going to be out a cool million if they didn't succeed in finding Cash Montgomery. If that meant that Sonny had to miss her plane and stay a few days longer in Colombia, then so be it. Life was full of inconveniences.

He drained the rest of his coffee and grimaced. *When did I get so grumpy?*

Besides, he'd already told her she could leave if she wanted to. She chose to stay. There had to be a reason she was sticking with the man who was hunting down her fugitive brother instead of just taking off on her own. She said she had no money left, but she may not have been telling him the truth.

Maybe she's hiding from something.

Yeah, that thought had occurred to him big-time over the past few hours while she and the baby were napping in the other room. The question was, what—or who— was she hiding from? And what did that have to do with Cash Montgomery?

Sonny had slept too long.

She only wished Ellie had, too. She'd checked the clock by the bed and saw that it was 3:00 a.m. Cooper was sound asleep in the next bed, breathing heavily as if she were deep into her REM state. Every so often, when the baby started to cry, Cooper stirred but didn't wake up.

That was good, Sonny decided. If she was going to get another crack at the computer, she was going to have to sneak out without Cooper knowing.

But first she had to rock Ellie to sleep again. It would be a long night for all of them if Ellie didn't sleep.

She wished she'd taken Baby 101 before she'd

insisted on coming down here. Serena had filled her in, and her mother had, too. But everything she'd done thus far had been a piece of cake compared to taking care of Ellie.

She recalled how she'd thought both her mother and her sister-in-law were making such a fuss. Sonny was female, after all. Shouldn't taking care of babies come naturally to all women?

Apparently not.

She rocked Ellie back and forth, trying to calm her crying. Do all mothers feel like complete imbeciles in the beginning stages of motherhood?

"Oh, sweet pea, your mamma is going to have my head on a spit if I don't take care of you properly," she crooned, nuzzling Ellie's pudgy wet cheeks.

Even as she said the words, she knew it wasn't true. Serena would be so happy to have this beautiful baby back in her arms that nothing else would matter, least of all any minor mistakes Sonny made along the way.

The baby continued to fuss in her arms. Afraid that she would wake up Cooper, Sonny grabbed the baby's blanket from the crib and went to the living room.

The light was on and the TV was turned down low. The screen showed an anchor speaking Spanish, talking about an upcoming festival. Sonny followed most of what he said although his dialect was different from the Spanish she knew. It didn't really matter what the news anchor said as long as it wasn't about the baby. She kept her ears open to any news of Eduardo Sanchez, though. She'd understand what that name meant for her in any language.

As she paced the living room in her bare feet, her

eyes drifted toward the kitchen. There was no light on, which meant that Marco had finally gone to bed. He kept the computer password protected, but that was easy enough for Sonny to get around. Even so, it would be risky to try now with Ellie still fussing. She didn't want to risk waking up the whole villa and getting caught again. Besides, she'd already sent out the important e-mail to her father. She could wait to see if he responded.

The look on Gil's face when he saw her standing at the computer was one she would never forget. His expression had been hard, his eyes cold and full of contempt. Sonny wasn't used to people looking at her that way and she hated even more that Gil had. But that didn't make any sense. Why would she care what he thought after what he'd done?

She wasn't perfect by any stretch of the imagination. She had a laundry list of flaws just like the next person. Stubbornness was up there at the top of the list.

Obviously she couldn't count taking Ellie as a flaw. Taking Ellie from her captors was completely fair, since Eduardo Sanchez had hired someone to pose as a maid in her sister-in-law's house, steal the baby and bring her to Colombia.

All of Sonny's actions since the kidnapping were firsts in her life. Who would've thought two months ago that she would travel to Colombia and work with Lucia, a former undercover agent, to rescue her niece from a high-ranking Colombian gangster? Those were things her brothers did. Not her.

Well, it certainly wasn't on any must-do-sometime-in-your-life list Sonny had ever written. And she hoped she never had to go through anything like the past few weeks again. She wasn't sure she could. But it had been worth it. Even as Ellie fussed in her arms and she dragged herself across the floor in exhaustion, she knew it was worth it to have Ellie out of Eduardo Sanchez's hands.

And then there was meeting Gil. Why did his disapproval of her matter so much? She shook her head. The man was downright annoying. "Lord, I have to be crazy for thinking this way," she said.

"Is something wrong?"

Sonny stopped short and swung around toward the sound of Gil's voice, continuing to rock Ellie in an effort to soothe her crying.

It wasn't working. The baby was rattled. So was Sonny.

Gil stood by the French doors leading outside, leaning up against the doorjamb. He was wearing a white T-shirt and loose-fitting blue jeans that had seen better days. His feet were bare and he held an empty mug on his index finger that was swaying back and forth. The warm Caribbean breeze filtered in, lifting the sheer drapes up into the room and gently messing up his hair as he stood there looking at her.

Her heart hammered wildly in her chest. It seemed odd that she hadn't noticed that the doors were open or that he was outside when she first walked into the living room. The flickering television should have given her a clue that *someone* was up. But her fatigue and preoccupation with the baby combined with all-consuming thoughts kept her from paying attention to those details. She'd have to make sure she was more on top of what she was doing so as not to be caught off guard again.

What is it about this man that keeps me so off balance?

"The baby okay?" he asked.

"I can't seem to get her to sleep." Admitting it made her feel as much a failure as she'd felt earlier, walking away from the airport.

"Is she still feeding during the night?"

"I'm not sure."

He raised his eyebrow as if to question her. It was a quick move. One that Sonny would've missed had she not been looking directly at him. And then it was gone. Tears sprang to her eyes. Who was she kidding?

"She might have colic."

Sonny looked at him skeptically. "How is it that you know so much about babies?"

Gil shrugged. "I lived in a house full of babies."

"Yours?"

That earned her a quick grin and a shake of Gil's head. "My mom and dad raised three of my younger cousins after my uncle and aunt died in a car accident when I was fifteen."

"Oh, how awful. I mean, the loss of your aunt and uncle. Not that they raised your cousins."

"I knew what you meant. You do what you have to do."

Sonny couldn't agree more. Why else had Serena trusted her to rescue her baby? It had to have taken an enormous amount of faith in the Lord on her part to trust Sonny that way. *You do what you have to do.*

"The two-bedroom ranch my parents owned was already too crowded, given that my room was the converted basement but the kids had to go somewhere so they came to live with us. My five-year-old cousin roomed with my sister upstairs. And I went from having my own room to having a baby and a three-year-old bunk with me.

"Johnny, the baby, had colic. I learned real quick how to take care of him so I could get a good night's sleep. He wasn't much older than Ellie when he came to live with us."

"Wow, five kids in two bedrooms."

Gil shrugged. "It wasn't so bad. Here, let me give it a try," he said. Strong, capable hands reached for the baby.

She was tired and it would have been easy to hand the baby over to someone with real experience. But she held back. "Why don't you show me?"

A flash of anger crossed his face and then it was gone. "You don't trust me."

"Trust is a big thing for me," she answered quietly.

"I'm sure it is."

Ellie was getting louder now.

"Sit right here with me while I hold her. I'm not going to steal her away."

Sonny realized then that she was holding Ellie tightly, as if she'd be snatched away at any moment. This is what it had come to, she realized. The fear Eduardo Sanchez and his cohorts had instilled in her—and her whole family—made it impossible to know who to trust.

His dark eyes searched hers. "What are you afraid of, Sonny?"

Reluctantly, she placed the crying baby in his arms. "You are going to stay in the room, right?"

With a crooked grin, he said, "Ellie's sticking with you, Sonny, because I don't do diapers."

She laughed nervously and settled into the seat near him, watching as he put the baby upright against his chest, resting her head on his shoulder. With long soothing strokes he rubbed Ellie's back. The baby continued to cry a little, but she was definitely calming down.

"Cute train pajamas," he said, examining the clothes Cooper had purchased earlier. "Not very little-girl-like."

"Cooper said there was slim pickings at the store. Wait until you see tomorrow's outfit. Ninja turtles."

Gil chuckled.

"I'm just grateful to have a change of clothes in case she spits up," Sonny said with a shrug.

She watched with admiration as Gil switched Ellie easily from one shoulder to the other.

"You *do* know babies," she said as Ellie finally stopped crying.

Gil smiled. "I never would have made it through high school if I hadn't figured this out."

She laughed and felt some of the tension inside her ease.

"When a baby has colic, it's best for them to sleep upright. I spent a lot of nights stretched out on an old recliner in the living room with Johnny on my chest."

"Why didn't your mother or father take care of the baby?"

He was quiet a moment, his expression tense as he leaned back against the sofa. "They had their own stuff to deal with," he said. "Mom was real close to my aunt. She took her death hard."

It was amazing. The man who had grilled her so doggedly earlier—who had refused to leave her be at the airport—was perfectly at home with Ellie in his arms.

"You're staring."

Startled, she looked away. "Am I?"

"Yes."

Heat crept up her cheeks. "I was just thinking how you could possibly be the same man I met at the airport."

"There's no difference, really. Just another face."

She wanted to say she liked this face better, but since he'd managed to get Ellie to sleep—her mouth slightly puckered open, her face so serene—she decided to keep it to herself.

"You want to say something." He wasn't asking a question, she noticed. He was probably reading her expression, which, given her tired state, was the equivalent of reading her mind.

"Thank you."

He frowned. "That's it? Nothing else?"

With a heavy sigh she said, "I'm so tired I can't even sleep."

He made a move to lean forward with the baby still on his shoulder. "Why don't you stretch out on the sofa? It's comfortable."

"No, that's okay."

Before she could protest further, he stood. Ellie seemed unaffected by his movement. "That's okay. I'll sit in the chair. You don't have to sleep if you don't want to. Just get comfortable. You look like you're about to fall over."

Gone were the cold stares and harsh attitude and in their place, Sonny saw concern. She welcomed the change, but she knew she shouldn't. Gil wanted something she couldn't give him. Something she didn't want him to get. As nice as he was now, she was sure the accusing glare would return if she didn't give him the information he wanted.

Walking over to the sofa, she perched on the edge. If she allowed herself to fall back against the deep cushions, she'd pass out. She was sure of it.

"Ellie's asleep," Sonny said. "Maybe I should put her back in the crib."

"Not yet. She needs to be fully asleep or she'll wake up again. Too bad we don't have a car seat to put her in," he said, easing back in the armchair.

"Why?"

"I used to let Johnny sleep in his car seat by my bed. It helped him."

"I could just hold her like you're doing."

Gil shook his head. "You're not used to holding her like this. If you fall asleep, she might slip from your arms."

Sonny sighed, annoyed with herself for thinking more about getting sleep than what she could do for the baby.

"I'm sorry."

The words were spoken so softly that Sonny would have missed them if she hadn't seen Gil's lips move. The expression on his face told her he meant it.

"What?"

"I'm sorry."

"Why?"

"I was wrong. I shouldn't have called you a criminal," he said gently.

Her smile was weak, but she felt it in her heart. "Forgiven."

"That easy, huh?"

"Yep, that easy. You got the baby to stop crying, so I'm in your debt for that."

He looked down into Ellie's face. "She doesn't look like you."

"She looks like my mother. Cash looks like my mother, too." Tears filled her eyes. How could she be complaining, even if only to herself, that she was tired and out of her element when Cash was the one so clearly in trouble?

"Come on," Gil urged. "You know you want to trust me."

It was true, but could she?

"Tell me what I want to hear, Sonny."

FIVE

"You never stop, do you?" she said, the weight of the day practically pulling on her eyelids. She was fighting to stay awake.

"No. But I can help you if you let me." His voice was sincere and made her yearn to let down her guard with him.

I trust in You, Lord, to guide me through my darkest hours. It would be so easy to trust Gil. But his motives for wanting information were mercenary.

"I don't know what you're talking about."

"I'm no fool, Sonny. This wasn't a quick vacation to Colombia. Why would Ellie's mother allow you to take her to a foreign country? And why didn't I ever see you with her until today? It doesn't make any sense."

She lifted her chin. "It doesn't need to make sense to you."

"Look, I know something is going on. I *can* help you. But only if you let me."

She turned away from his probing gaze. "You already 'helped' me back at the airport," she said sarcastically. "Or have you already forgotten that?"

"You're terrified of something."

"How do you know it's not you?"

He took in her words and considered them. "Fair enough. But I know what kind of trouble your brother was in. If you're afraid—"

She cut him off. "I told you all I know."

"Have you?"

Running her fingers through her hair in frustration, she shifted her position on the sofa. "Obviously, you still don't believe me."

"I believe what you've told me is true. But I don't believe you've told me everything."

She bit her lip. "You want something I can't give you."

"Cash."

She nodded. "I don't know where he is."

"Then why did you come here? And why do you have his baby, a baby you don't even know how to take care of?"

His words, however true, stung. She closed her eyes for a brief moment to hold back her tears. A good cry was long overdue. She hadn't really allowed herself that for fear she'd never recover enough to do what she had to do.

"Do you know who can find your brother?"

Eduardo Sanchez could give Gil a whole lot of information. But she didn't want Gil or his team to mess with the Colombian kingpin. Or connect anyone in her family to him. At least not until she and Ellie were in the United States again.

When she didn't answer, he went on in a quiet voice. "Your loyalty to your brother is admirable. It's clear by your actions that you love him very much. But you're not doing Cash or yourself any favors. He needs to come out of hiding."

"You don't even know me or my family. How can you make a claim like that?"

"He was arrested for a crime and if you cared for him like you say you do, you'd make sure he was brought in for justice."

She laughed humorlessly. "Is that why you're doing this? For justice? Don't even go there, Gil. I know what you're after. Money. Isn't that what all bounty hunters are after?"

His eyes darkened for a brief moment. "I'm not going to lie to you. I get paid well for bringing criminals back in to face trial. But I want justice, too."

"For who?"

"For the people."

She shook her head. "You don't know anything about this case, do you? All you know is there's a nice bounty up for grabs."

"I don't need to know all the details. I know that bail was set at one million dollars and judges don't issue that kind of bail without a good reason. DEA or not, there had to be compelling proof for the judge to set bail so high. Your loyalty and love for your brother don't change the fact that he's guilty of a crime."

It was hard to sit still with Gil talking about Cash as if he was a common street thug. "You've been out of the country too long, Gil. In America, a person is innocent until proven guilty. You've forgotten that."

Their eyes met. Sonny liked his eyes. When he wasn't being hard and accusing, his eyes were warm and she found herself drifting away from all that was happening, focusing on the depth of his gaze instead of the stress of the past few weeks.

Instead of the words he was saying.

She shook the thoughts out of her mind. She was tired. And she was sure he was using that to get her to talk. She couldn't allow herself to be trumped in a battle of wills.

"You're right," he finally said. "But Cash can't prove his innocence unless he comes in."

"I couldn't agree more. And believe it or not, we want the same thing."

"Do we?" He scanned her face intently, looking into her eyes, then at her lips, then back to her eyes.

"Yes," she said, shaking away the fluttering feeling in her stomach. "I miss my brother. Despite what you think, I'd like nothing better than for him to come home. His wife, Serena, feels the same way. And before you start thinking you can grill her, she's not in Colombia. And she doesn't know where he is, either."

"Then trust me. Help me find him."

"I have put my trust in others that justice will be served."

Gil cocked his head to one side. "Others? Who?"

"The Lord."

He made a noise of frustration. "You'd be foolish to wait around for miracles, Sonny."

"Why? You don't think the Lord will answer my prayers?"

"I think prayer helps a person get through hard times, but it's not a lottery ticket."

She laughed softly. "No, you're right. But I can't look at that baby sleeping soundly in your arms right now and not believe in miracles. They happen every day all around us, whether we see them or not.

"My faith in God is not just something I do on a Sunday morning at church, Gil. My faith is the backbone of my family's life and mine. It's my driving force."

Gil made no reply.

Sonny's cheeks flamed and she found it hard to turn away from his intent stare. She couldn't tell him that when their eyes met it made her heart skip a beat. Men didn't do that to Sonny. At least, no man she'd ever known had.

All the men she'd encountered at work were not men she wanted to date. And although Mrs. Altman, the church organist, was always trying to fix her up with one eligible Christian bachelor or another, she never found any man interesting enough to pursue beyond a first date. She often ended up turning the relationship into a good friendship.

Sonny had only just met Gil. But she'd never been this attracted to a man before. Especially a man who couldn't be more wrong for her if he tried.

Lord, are you trying to tell me something? Because if You are, I'm not getting it.

She shrugged the feeling off. "You remind me of..."

"Who?" he asked.

"My brother."

"Cash?"

She shook her head. "No, Dylan. He's the oldest. Cash is a few years younger. It took Mom and Dad a while to have me."

"I'm sure they were a handful when they were kids."

"Yeah, I guess."

"Why do I remind you of your brother?"

They say that if you have a good relationship with your father and your brothers, you look for a man who reminds you of them. Sonny supposed that was why she was suddenly feeling drawn to Gil.

"He's gruff, like you. All big, bad, tough guy on the outside, you know?"

She could tell he wanted to laugh out loud. A funny sound escaped his lips, but he held back to keep from waking the baby. His chest rocked up and down as he laughed silently.

"And you willingly handed the baby over anyway?" he finally said.

"That's just it. Dylan always comes across like the big, bad marine. He's a cop now. But when you get him in a room full of my little cousins during the holidays, he's just a cream puff. He's the one they all flock to. He rolls around on the floor and plays with them, makes them laugh. They never leave him alone. But he doesn't mind. He's just a big kid behind that gruff exterior."

"You think that's what I'm like?"

"Are you telling me you're not?"

"You don't know me."

"I know what I see," she said, gesturing to Ellie, who was completely content on his shoulder. "You just told me you used to rock your little cousin to sleep at night and now you're holding Ellie like she was made to fit in your arms. You're a softy, Gil."

"Appearances can be deceiving, Sonny. I'm still going to bring your brother in when I find him."

She nodded, irritated that his determination to collect

his bounty had crept into the conversation. The two of them would always be at odds on that matter. The very last thing Sonny would help Gil with was looking for Cash if it meant he'd interfere with the rescue operation.

"You may want the world to believe you're a hard case, some of us know better, Gil."

He shifted in the chair. "Listen, Sonny. Whatever game you're playing with me, you can stop. Smooth talking isn't going to keep me from doing my job."

She tried not to show how his accusation hurt. "I wasn't playing a game. What I said was a compliment."

He nodded, apparently somewhat thrown by her sincerity. "Then thank you. But you should know that Marco is going to figure out what you did online. And when he does, we'll find your brother."

No, you won't, Sonny thought. She'd made sure she didn't even mention Cash's name in her e-mail to her father. If only she'd had time, she would have planted something to steer them off course in case they did find her e-mail.

Sonny hadn't had time to think when Gil and Marco had left to get the crib. She just knew that she had to alert her father and enlist his help in getting out of Colombia with Ellie. It was only a matter of time before Eduardo Sanchez started searching.

Neither Gil nor his team knew what kind of monster they were dealing with. He was just the CEO of a shipping company to them. But Sonny knew all too well. If they didn't move fast, they probably wouldn't be able to use Ellie's passport to leave by plane. In fact, it might already be too late. Eduardo Sanchez was a powerful man in Colombia. He rose above the law, despite his illegal dealings. To many, he was a king for bringing small hill towns out of poverty and filtering money—despite the illegal means in which he acquired it—back to communities in need.

By the standards of many, he was living a good Christian life. But his motives had nothing to do with helping others and everything to do with control and power.

Gil was worried about finding an e-mail containing information about Cash. But that was the least of his worries. He just didn't know it yet.

"You know, my father must have been devastated when the plane landed and Ellie and I weren't on it." Oh, how she wanted to be able to call him to let him know they were both all right. But she couldn't do that without someone hearing the conversation. And that would only bring on a new onslaught of questions from Gil and his team. Sonny wasn't ready to deal with that.

She realized that it was a good thing she knew nothing about what was going on with Dylan and his former military team in regards to Cash's rescue. She was feeling worn down, and knew that she might let something slip if Gil started grilling her again. Fortunately, she had no idea what was going on with Dylan and Cash. Dylan had been right to keep the plans from her.

"For a woman who values her faith so highly, you must be having a crisis of conscience."

Gil's words broke into her thoughts. "Why do you say that?"

"You were sitting there looking…guilty, actually. Clearly you're upset."

He'd misread her expression. *Good.* "You still think I'm guilty of something?"

"You tell me. Why did you come to Colombia, Sonny? Your passport shows you boarded a plane in Chicago and yet you were headed to Miami."

Anger surged through her. "You went through my things?"

"Cooper did. But we already knew about the plane tickets so she didn't find anything of real interest."

"You tapped into the airline's computer to spy on me? How dare you!"

Her voice was loud enough to startle Ellie, but the baby didn't fully rouse.

"If you want to get back to sleep any time soon, I'd keep your voice low." He patted Ellie's back lightly until she settled again. "Marco checked you out before your plane ever hit the tarmac here in South America."

Her jaw nearly hit the floor. "You've been following me since before I got here?"

"I'm good at what I do, Sonny. That's why the bonds-man pays me."

"Money."

She hadn't meant for her voice to sound so accusing, but this was her brother they were talking about. Not some jackpot at a church bingo game.

"I'm not out to hurt you."

"You already did."

A flash of alarm crossed his face. Then he looked at her quizzically.

"You interfered with my leaving Colombia when I needed to get home," she reminded him.

"As soon as you tell me how I can find your brother, I'll put you on the plane myself."

Sonny balled her fists and leaped from the sofa. She had to release some of the frustration that had been building inside her since long before she'd even set foot in Colombia. Since before Cash had gotten into the mess he was in.

The problem was she really didn't know how far to go back, but pacing the floor wasn't going to give her the answers she longed for. She wanted to know her brother was alive. She wanted to believe that she and Ellie would get back to the United States safely.

Even though Gil was trying to reassure her and get her to trust him, she knew he didn't have those answers, either.

"You just don't get it. You really don't understand how you've endangered all of us."

"All of us? Why don't you tell me, Sonny. Then I'll understand. Because right now you're talking riddles. What are you hiding?"

SIX

The burden was as heavy as her fatigue, weighing her down so that her shoulders ached. *Lord, give me strength. Don't allow me to be blinded by this man.*

"I'm tired," she said, folding her arms across her chest.

Gil's face showed resignation and perhaps a little disappointment. His face was drawn and his eyelids were heavy. He was tired, as well, and probably fed up with her silence, too.

He held her steady with his stare. She could look at him all night, she decided. Gil had a way about him, that was for sure. Especially as he sat there with the baby in his arms.

"What's holding you back, Sonny?" he finally asked.

She answered honestly. "I can't risk it." Her voice was low, even to her own ears.

He implored her with his eyes. When she said no more, he said, "Sonny, if we're all in danger now, you need to come clean. This isn't just about you and Ellie anymore."

Sonny simply nodded.

"I think she'll sleep fine now," he said, easing himself to the end of the chair.

"Thank you." Whether or not he understood her thanks were for his not pressing her any further, she didn't know. All she did know was that if she didn't get some sleep, she'd burst into a million tears and truly be at Gil's mercy.

Sonny found herself longing to have him hold her as gently as he'd held the baby in his strong, capable arms. She felt as if she were a piece of fragile glass that could break at any moment.

She didn't try to take the baby from him. Instead, Gil followed her to the bedroom. She opened the door slowly, allowing the light from the living room to spill into the darkness, showing the way to the crib. In one smooth, gentle move, he settled Ellie into the crib, covering her with the blanket.

He turned to Sonny. The light from the living room shone bright in his dark eyes, making them glow. A shadow was cast over half his face, but she could see clearly his strong, square jaw and wavy dark hair. Her hands itched to touch the locks of hair falling across his forehead as he looked down at her.

As their eyes locked, the air in the room seemed to disappear.

"Good night, Sonny," he whispered.

She closed her eyes as he moved past her. The scent of him filled her senses. He smelled clean like soap and fresh air. It was a heady scent that made her lightheaded.

When Gil closed the door behind him, Sonny dropped to her knees by the bed. The room was dark. The baby and Cooper were asleep. She was alone with her thoughts.

She'd never felt the need to kneel while praying. But tonight she felt her strength slipping away and she needed help.

In the darkness her eyes filled with tears. She didn't speak her prayer out loud, but rather let the words run through her mind as she asked the Lord how she could be so attracted to a man who wanted to cause harm to someone she loved so dearly.

I am losing it. Gil walked across the cool tiled floor in his bare feet, picked up the remote and turned off the television. He was dead on his feet.

He'd hardly slept more than four hours a night in the past few weeks. But he knew if he climbed into his bed, he'd just be watching the red digital numbers on the clock until light crept in through the window.

The woman had him rattled. That was for sure. Maybe he'd been at this job way too long. If Sonny Montgomery could smooth his edge, steal his focus and distract him from the process of bringing in a criminal, he was losing it. How effective could he be as a bounty hunter if he spent his time looking at her upturned nose and the freckles on her cheeks?

"Real professional, Gil. Nice work," he chided himself as he rearranged the pillows on the sofa, punching them down. Then he stretched himself out on the length of the couch.

He wasn't even going to think about why he was noticing freckles on a woman he was sure was in trouble up to her baby-blue eyes. *And they were truly magnificent eyes.*

He sputtered at the thought. "So she has pretty eyes,"

he said quietly, glancing at the bedroom door. "They're just eyes."

But she had kissed him. He couldn't even put into words how much the kiss had surprised him…and affected him. Granted, there was nothing intimate about the kiss. He knew that. But the look on her face as she'd stood on tiptoe to reach him—the connection he'd made with her eyes and the feel of her lips on his—was still very much in his mind. It played over and over again.

That was why he couldn't sleep. How could a man sleep with a face like Sonny Montgomery's running through his mind?

Gil shook his head, muttering, "Women." Sighing, he looked up at the ceiling. "Is this supposed to mean something?"

Startled by his action, he tensed. Gil hadn't had the Lord in his life for more years than he could count.

There'd never been a definite breaking away from his faith. Things had faded away when his mom lost her sister. She stopped going to church. Stopped doing the things she'd always loved doing.

Despite his concern, his father had never pushed the issue and eventually his mom began going back to church again. But that wasn't until after Gil had left for the army. By then Gil's relationship with God had taken a backseat to everything else in his life.

Funny how a few short hours with a Christian woman who wasn't afraid to show her faith had him falling into old habits. He couldn't exactly say that it bothered him. It was actually a breath of fresh air.

"Is this Your way of getting my attention?"

Gil didn't expect an answer. He knew better. But as

his dad had always said, putting the words out there was how you made the connection. No telephone required to talk to the Lord, he remembered his dad telling him before he'd gotten on the plane for boot camp. Just close your eyes and He'll listen.

Gil needed to wipe the image of Sonny from his brain as best he could. Pulling the blanket from the back of the sofa, he covered himself, rolled to his side and closed his eyes.

She was still there in his mind. Somehow she'd gotten under his skin. Who was he kidding? He wasn't going to sleep at all tonight.

He tried to focus on work. Gil was sure Sonny had been trying to steer him the wrong way earlier when she'd been on the computer. Marco had to work his magic and find that e-mail.

"That's right," he muttered. "Keep your mind on the job, not the woman."

If Sonny had sent a message to warn her brother that Gil and his team were on to him, Marco would find it. And Gil would use it to find Cash. No matter how much the image of Cash's little sister kept Gil tossing tonight.

"Yo, Gil." His body shook as if he was in the middle of an earthquake. "Dude, wake up!"

Reluctant to be pulled from the comfortable position he'd been sleeping in, Gil opened one eye. It refused to stay open. "What is it? What's happened?" he said in a raspy, sleep-filled voice. Hadn't he just fallen asleep?

He was vaguely aware that the earth had stopped moving and it dawned on him that Cooper had been shaking him awake. He took a moment to position himself upright and fully open his eyes.

"You were sleeping like you were dead. Marco's been calling you from the kitchen for at least five minutes and you didn't so much as twitch," Cooper said, sitting back on the other end of the sofa. "He's got something."

That kicked Gil into gear. He rubbed his hands over his face. When he found the strength to stand up, he was stopped by the look on Cooper's face.

"Is it good or bad?"

She shrugged. "Not sure yet. Go talk to Marco."

Gil went to the kitchen, his bare feet cold on the tiled floor. He found Marco perched on a stool, typing furiously and poring through pages of printout.

"She's good. I'll give her that. She managed to send an e-mail and cover her tracks—mostly—in that short amount of time we were gone. She left an imprint."

"Good. Did she e-mail Cash?" He felt a rush of disappointment. Even though Gil wanted to find information about Cash, part of him hoped that Sonny had been telling the truth about the computer.

"I hope not. If she did, we are in the wrong country."

Gil frowned. "How do you know?"

"I was able to track her e-mail by following the IP address. Don't ask me how or I'll have to plead the Fifth Amendment. Or kill you. Take your pick," Marco said with a laugh.

"Just tell me where it ended up."

"A hotel in Miami. It went through a dedicated line, so my guess is it was picked up at the hotel's business center."

"She was taking a plane to Miami," Gil said,

suddenly wondering who else besides her father might be meeting her there. His mind immediately shifted to whether or not Sonny was meeting a boyfriend. She was, after all, a beautiful woman. Just because Marco hadn't uncovered any information about Sonny's involvements didn't mean she didn't have any. It just meant that Marco hadn't looked deep enough.

Until this moment, it hadn't mattered to Gil. What did he care if she had a boyfriend? But now, that little bit of information was something he needed to know.

"The e-mail didn't say much. Kind of cryptic, if you ask me," Marco said, pulling it up on the screen.

"What did it say?"

"It said, 'Detained, Dad. Tell Serena we'll both be home for her birthday. I'll be in touch.'"

Gil stared at the words on the screen. "That's it?"

"That's it. Probably all she had time for. Who do you think the 'we' is?"

"Guys!" Cooper called from the other room.

With a brief glance toward Cooper, Gil answered, "Ellie, I suppose."

"Gillespie! You're going to want to see this!"

The urgent sound of Cooper's voice drew Gil and Marco to the living room. Cooper was on the sofa with the remote in her hand, staring intently at the television. Her face was ashen.

"What's going on?"

"Ah, maybe nothing. But there's some big brouhaha over a missing baby. Some businessman says his baby was taken from her crib in the early morning *yesterday*. Didn't you say you hadn't seen Sonny with a baby before yesterday?"

A dull ache began to grow in the pit of his stomach. "Yeah."

Of the three of them, Cooper was most fluent in Spanish, so she translated as the news anchor talked.

"Eduardo Sanchez and his wife adopted a baby girl three months ago after trying unsuccessfully to have a child of their own. Early yesterday morning someone entered their estate and took the child." Cooper looked at the guys. "They aren't showing a picture of the baby," she said.

Gil turned away from the television and stared at the bedroom where Sonny and Ellie were still sleeping. "Do we really need one?"

"You think they're talking about Ellie?" Marco asked.

"No way," Cooper said, her eyes wide with alarm. "You think she stole the kid?"

Was it just coincidence that Eduardo Sanchez's baby disappeared on the same morning that Ellie magically appeared with Sonny? Gil didn't like coincidences.

"You said Eduardo Sanchez was a businessman? What business?" Gil asked.

"You'll like this," Cooper said. "Aztec Corporation."

"Sonny knows something she's trying real hard to keep from us and I'm not waiting any longer to find out what that is. Sonny?" he called, banging on the bedroom door.

Cooper bolted from the sofa. "You're going to wake up the entire complex. Let me get her."

But before Cooper could go into the bedroom, the door opened.

"What is your problem?" Sonny said. "Ellie's sleeping.

And after the night I had with her, I'd just as soon keep it that way for a while."

"Come here."

Gil ignored the fact that her hair was wet and she smelled fresh like baby powder. Fighting all his senses, he took Sonny by the arm and dragged her into the living room.

"I have to dry my hair."

"It can wait."

"Obviously you don't have unruly hair or you wouldn't suggest such a thing," Sonny said, joking with him.

Gil pointed to the television. "What's this all about?"

"You tell me."

Sonny stared at the television while a fierce-looking Eduardo Sanchez pounded on a podium and spoke of the kidnapping.

She turned and faced Gil, her expression unreadable. "I have no idea."

"Don't give me that. You spoke Spanish perfectly yesterday. You know what he's saying."

She cocked her head to one side. "Yes, I know what this man is saying. He's saying his baby has been kidnapped. But why should that matter to me? I don't know where his baby is."

"Why don't I believe you?"

She blew out a quick breath. "Gee, I don't know. Maybe you weren't hugged enough as a kid."

"Cute. Now give me a straight answer."

Sonny fought the urge to take a step back. Gil's hard accusing stare was back, boring into her. He was right, of course. She'd known this would happen eventually. She'd just hoped Eduardo Sanchez wouldn't be brazen enough to announce the baby's disappearance on the news.

When she stared at the Colombian kingpin's face on the television screen, she had to hold her emotions at bay. In his native Spanish, he addressed the camera, looking directly at it, almost as if he could reach through the camera and grab her. *"This crime is unconscionable."* He said. *"I promise you, whoever took my daughter will pay to the full extent of the law."*

Being the powerful man that Sanchez was in Colombia, no one would question whether or not the baby he'd recently acquired was adopted legally. They'd all just assume the paperwork was in perfect order. Nice and tidy.

Except it wasn't. It was absolutely illegal.

If it came down to it, Sonny had no doubt Eduardo Sanchez would exact his own justice. Her hands were shaking and she fought desperately to still them to avoid giving herself away. How much Gil and his team knew about the kidnapping and how it related to her family, she had no idea. They knew about the Aztec Corporation. Did they already know that Eduardo Sanchez headed up the Aztec Corporation? Sonny was determined not to give up any more information than she had to until absolutely necessary but that look on Gil's face told her it was going to be a challenge.

Gil propped his hands on his hips. "Okay, put it to me plainly. Is Ellie the baby they're looking for?"

Her heart hammered in her chest and when his expression collapsed, she knew she didn't have to utter a word. Her face gave her away. So much for not giving up information.

Gil charged toward the bedroom with Sonny on his heels.

"Don't go in there, Gil. Please, leave her alone."

Gil ignored Sonny's plea and pushed the door open.

"Gil, she's asleep," she implored him. "Please don't take her."

Tears stung her eyes and her breath caught in her throat. She charged passed him and scooped Ellie up into her arms before he got to the crib. The baby, who had been sound asleep after her morning feeding and bath, was now crying loud and hard because she'd been woken up so abruptly.

"She's my brother's baby, Gil," she said. "She doesn't belong to Eduardo Sanchez."

"If that were true—"

"It is!"

"—you would have contacted the authorities and let them handle it."

"They won't help, Gil! It's too complicated!"

He looked at the baby for a long moment and then switched his gaze to Sonny. His voice was low and measured as he spoke. "You didn't come to Colombia with this baby, Sonny. You came alone. You boarded a flight in Chicago, made a transfer in Houston and then again in Panama City before landing in Bogotá. I know this because I was on that plane with you. You never knew I was there."

"You were on the plane?"

"And then I followed you to Monteria. Not once did I see you in the marketplace with Ellie. I only saw you with her at the airport. Yesterday. The same day Eduardo Sanchez's baby disappeared."

"Gil, listen to me. She's my brother's baby."

He took a step forward; she countered by stepping back. "Did you take her?"

"She's my niece."

Sonny turned from him, trying to soothe Ellie as well as her rampant heart, but the tears she'd been holding back broke free and ran down her face.

Please, Lord, give me a sign. Help me figure out what to do.

She had no idea how to get out of Colombia now that Eduardo Sanchez had rallied his troops and made a publicity stunt out of the kidnapping. They were sure to be looking for a baby at the airport, so Ellie's newly acquired passport was now useless. Even if there were no photos of her on the news, the authorities would surely have some, supplied by Sanchez himself.

Gil placed a gentle hand on her shoulder, but he kept his distance. "Talk to me, Sonny. You have to tell me everything."

How could she trust him? How could she take that chance when she knew his goal was to find Cash?

But, Lord, I know I can't do this alone.

"Gil, I need your help. It doesn't matter how I got her. The only thing that matters is that her name is Ellie Montgomery."

"Did you steal that baby from Eduardo Sanchez's estate?" Marco said from the doorway, his mouth open wide in horror.

Gil put up a hand to quiet him.

"Oh, this is bad, Gil. Real bad," Cooper said, shaking her head. "If we get caught with that baby…"

"Answer me, Sonny. Did you take this baby?"

Sonny swung around to face Gil. "Yes."

The room was silent. But for the gentle breeze scraping an errant branch against the window, there was no sound. Even Ellie remained quiet.

Eyes as wide as saucers, Gil said, "You kidnapped her?"

"Since she never belong to Eduardo Sanchez in the first place, it wasn't kidnapping. *He* kidnapped *her* from America."

"Really? Tell that to Eduardo Sanchez and the authorities," Marco said.

"I didn't do it alone."

Gil put his hand on his forehead as he thought. "I was following you. How could you have taken her? You never left your room until yesterday morning."

"Which is when she took her," Marco said.

"That's when I lost you. It was only after Marco hacked the airline's site that I found out you were leaving Colombia via Monteria, not Bogotá."

"I told you. I didn't do it alone."

"Who helped you? Cash?" Gil didn't take his eyes off her. She wanted desperately to know what he was thinking. Did he believe her or despise her? In those few seconds, she wanted to trust him more than anything.

As she stifled a sob, she said, "I don't know where Cash is. I wish I did. You have to believe me, Gil."

Cooper swallowed hard. "Gil, what are we going to do?"

He sighed, but never looked away from Sonny.

Sonny held his gaze, searching his eyes, looking for any kind of sign that would let her know he was on her side. That she could finally trust him.

"Cooper, go listen to the broadcast. See if there's any information we can use."

"Gil—" Cooper said in protest.

"Just do it, please."

He turned to Sonny. "How'd you get her out of the estate, Sonny? How'd you get in, for that matter? Eduardo Sanchez looks to be a powerful man. There had to be guards all over the place."

His scrutiny nearly broke her heart. Gone was the gentle man who'd held Ellie so delicately last night. In his eyes, Sonny had stolen another man's child. That's all he cared about. She *was* a criminal after all, no better than what he thought of her brother.

She wanted to drop to the floor and weep.

"Uh, Gil, what are you thinking?" Marco said, looking pale. "Cuz, I don't have to tell you it would be bad for us to get caught up in a kidnapping. Really bad."

Sonny suddenly recalled a prayer her mother had said to her before she left for Colombia. *They that hope in the Lord will renew their strength, they will soar as with eagles' wings; they will run and not grow weary, walk and not grow faint.* And then her mother had said, "Go soar, Sonny."

Her mother had faith in her and she had to draw strength from that faith now. It was almost as if she'd known Sonny would need this verse at some point to keep her going.

Drawing a renewing breath of air into her lungs, she focused on being calm and strong.

At any moment, one of them could pick up the telephone, call the Colombian authorities and end this whole thing. Ellie would be returned to Sanchez's estate and kept so heavily guarded that it would be impossible to rescue her from the kingpin's clutches again. Sonny would be hauled off to some Colombian prison. *If I'm lucky, I'll end up in prison. I could end up disappearing without a trace.*

Sonny licked her lips and tried to ignore Ellie's crying as she held her tightly. She kept her voice even as she spoke.

"Marco, go online and check out Eduardo Sanchez. Not like you're looking for a phone number in the white pages. Like you did when you were looking for information about me. Like you did for my brother Cash. And while you're at it, add one more name to the list. Manuel Turgis."

"Who's that?" Gil asked.

"Sanchez's partner. I assure you it will make for interesting reading. Then you'll believe me when I say I am taking *my* niece home to the United States to *her* mother."

"Gil?" Marco said.

"Do it." Gil turned back to Sonny, his voice suddenly harsh. "What's it going to say, Sonny? What kind of men have you gotten yourself involved with?"

She shook her head. "Not me. This association was formed long before I was born."

His brow knitted. "I don't understand."

"Gil, I don't have the energy to take your grilling," she pleaded. "Just check it out. I'll answer every question you ask after."

Gil looked angry, as if he'd been betrayed. How he could believe she'd betrayed him was beyond her comprehension. He was the one who'd interfered with her plans to leave Colombia with Ellie in the first place. But he stared at her as if she'd somehow done him wrong instead of the other way around.

"You both could have been killed," he said quietly. He held himself rigid, his back straight, his arms stiff by his sides. As if it was taking every bit of strength he had to hold himself in reserve. "How could you put her in danger this way?"

Sonny's mouth dropped open. "Me? Need I remind you that if you hadn't interfered we'd be in Miami right now?"

"With who, Cash?"

She rolled her eyes. "You're still more concerned with finding my brother than anything else. You'll have to collect your precious bounty on your own, Gil. I don't know where Cash is. I've told you that countless times."

"If you did know, would you tell me?"

She hesitated for a split second. "No. I've told you that already, too."

Gil spun on his heels and pushed past Marco, who was still standing in the doorway.

"What are you going to do, Gil?" Sonny asked, frantic.

He said nothing. Ellie was now wailing so loudly Sonny thought her head was about to explode. The tears in her eyes made it hard to see.

"Let me take the baby," Cooper said quietly, coming up beside her.

"No!" She held the baby tighter. "Gil, answer me!"

Cooper put out her arms. "Sonny, give me the baby."

"Please don't take her to the authorities," Sonny cried. "You can't do that!" *Oh, Lord, please don't let them take her away!*

Cooper gripped Sonny by the shoulders. "You're upset. You're going to hurt Ellie if you don't ease up."

Sonny glanced down and realized she was holding Ellie in a death grip.

Sonny charged into the living room behind Gil, who was pacing around the sofa as if it helped him think.

"You can't take her away from me," she pleaded. "She belongs with her mother. She belongs in America, not in Colombia. Anyone could take one look at her and see that she's my brother's child."

Gil saw the struggle Sonny was having with Cooper and advanced toward them.

He spoke calmly, looking directly in her eyes. "Give the baby to Cooper to hold, Sonny."

"Please, Gil. Please! Don't take her away!"

SEVEN

"Take it easy, Sonny. I'm not going to hand Ellie over to anyone," Gil said. "I'm just letting Cooper hold her because you're upset."

Sonny gulped back a sob and then nodded.

As Gil took Ellie from Sonny and handed her over to Cooper, Sonny felt as if her arms were being ripped from her body.

The loud rumble of an engine drew Gil's attention outside. He strode quickly to the window, pulled the curtain aside and peered out.

"What is it?" Cooper asked, shifting the baby in her arms. "What's that sound?"

"Military trucks. As in more than just a few."

"Whoa," Marco said. "Um, damage control, Gil? We need some."

Gil let the curtain fall back into place. "Let's not get paranoid. This is Colombia after all. There are a lot of reasons why military vehicles roam these streets. It doesn't necessarily have anything to do with what's happened here."

Marco sputtered. "Come on, boss. If Sanchez is as big a deal as the news report says, he probably has the whole country combing the streets for this baby. It sounds like he has the clout to do it."

Gil considered what Marco said. "If they're looking for the baby, they don't know she's here. At least not yet. They're probably all over every city with an international airport."

"How do you know they're after the baby? I mean, Eduardo Sanchez is a businessman. He's not military," Cooper said.

Gil turned to Sonny. "You want to fill us in on what you know about Eduardo Sanchez? And what was the other name?"

"Manuel Turgis," Sonny said, her heartbeat beginning to slow down.

"Who are these people?"

"They're part of the Aztec Corporation."

Gil shook his head in frustration. "Don't play with me, Sonny. I don't want their résumés. We know Sanchez is the CEO of Aztec. But who is he to you and how is it that he came into possession of your *niece?*"

Shoulders sagging, Sonny said, "You're determined to prove that Cash and I are criminals, aren't you?"

She reached toward the fussing baby in Cooper's arms, touching her hand and stroking her cheek. She wasn't sure if she was trying to comfort the baby or herself.

"Give me a reason not to," Gil said.

And he meant it. He couldn't remember a time when he wanted to believe he was wrong more than right now.

He couldn't be involved with a criminal. He wouldn't. It went against everything he believed in. The fact that he even entertained the notion last night went against every professional ethic he held dear. Instead of accepting the facts that were right in front of him, he wanted her to prove that he was right to feel…whatever it was he was feeling for her.

He held his position, searching her face—her incredible eyes—as she looked back at him. He had to give her points for not running away from the pressure that threatened to explode in the room, from the weight of Marco's and Cooper's furious stares. But then again, she'd already proven how tough she could be back at the airport.

"We're not criminals, Gil. I could tell the whole story, but you probably still won't believe me." Her voice was quiet and it dawned on him that she wasn't going to feel free to talk until Ellie was back in her crib.

"Try me."

She sighed as if the weight of the world were dragging her down.

"My brother was framed by people in the Aztec Corporation. He got too close to the truth."

"The truth about what? Drugs?"

Sonny shook her head. "Despite the 'evidence' they found in Cash's apartment in Chicago when he was arrested, it wasn't drugs. It was never drugs. But that's what Manuel Turgis wanted the Feds to think—that the reason Cash was coming to Colombia was for drugs.

"Cash married a woman named Serena Davco in a secret ceremony—Dylan and I didn't even know about it. Neither did our parents. Her family, specifically her father, Byron Davco, was working with Turgis to launder money and stolen valuables."

Gil instinctively reached out and rumpled the downy

hair on Ellie's head as she wriggled in Cooper's arms. "What kind of valuables?"

"Stolen Aztec artifacts from Mexico. One of the Aztec Corporation's businesses is making replicas of ancient art and selling them worldwide. But they also sell the real stuff along with stolen artwork on the black market."

"They deal in art? What kind?" Cooper asked, bouncing Ellie up and down.

"Paintings. Byron double-crossed Turgis in a deal nearly thirty years ago. Turgis retaliated by going after Byron's family. He killed Byron's wife in a fire. Serena and her younger sister, Tammie, nearly died."

Sonny eased into a chair. "Three priceless paintings had been stolen and painted over to conceal them while they were being shipped. Eduardo Sanchez paid to have the paintings sent to a European buyer. The money was transferred to a Swiss account. But the deal fell through the night Serena's mother was killed in the fire at the family mansion."

"What happened?" Gil asked.

"Serena's mother found out that Byron was dealing with Turgis to launder money. She took the information Byron needed to complete the transaction and threatened to give it to the authorities. Turgis found out and knew he couldn't let that happen, so he murdered Serena's mother. Until that time he'd been operating in the United States without any FBI interest. Unfortunately, the number to the Swiss account and the whereabouts of the last painting were lost in the fire."

Gil rubbed his hand over his face. "That couldn't have gone over well with Turgis's boss."

"It didn't. Eduardo Sanchez was furious because it

put his operation at risk and blackened his name. He took it out on Turgis, who then vowed to destroy Byron Davco. He has waged a war against Serena's family ever since, killing those associated with Byron Davco unless he paid money for their protection."

"He extorted money from Davco for thirty years?" Gil asked. "What changed?"

"Byron has Alzheimer's. When he could no longer pay, Turgis went after Serena. You see, Eduardo Sanchez and Manuel Turgis believed that Byron knew where that last painting was. It was a matter of pride and greed that drove them all these years. Manuel Turgis was humiliated among his people that the deal never went through. He needed to make good on his word to Eduardo Sanchez. Sanchez never let him forget how he botched the deal and in turn, they never let Byron Davco forget his part in it. To cut their losses and let it go would have made them appear weak. So they terrorized Byron and his family, hoping to find that last painting."

"You say it was the last painting?"

"Yes. Cash knew about it. When the statute of limitations was up on the theft, the painting appeared on the open market for auction, opening up an old wound and an unsettled debt that infuriated Eduardo Sanchez."

Marco stood by the door to the kitchen, listening with interest. "Is that when Ellie was taken?"

"Yes," Sonny said, her eyes filling with tears. "When Cash realized just how dangerous the situation was with Sanchez and Turgis, he decided not to involve his family. He never told us about Serena or Ellie. Not until it was too late and Ellie had been taken."

She turned in her seat and looked directly at Gil. "My

brother isn't what the authorities make him out to be. He didn't jump bail because he's guilty of anything. He came here to rescue his daughter."

"And was kidnapped himself in the process?" Gil asked.

Sonny laughed wryly. "You still don't believe me."

"Would you?"

She thought a moment. "Maybe not. But if you check out Manuel Turgis and Eduardo Sanchez, you'll find out enough to realize I'm telling you the truth."

A tear trickled down Sonny's cheek. Gil had a strong urge to reach over and brush it away. Sonny looked beaten down. Whatever she'd been through these past few months had taken its toll on her.

He forced his gaze away from her face. "The baby's hungry," he said, nodding his head at Ellie, who was gumming her fist.

Sonny rubbed her temple. "She needs a bottle."

"Get Ellie back to sleep and then we can talk more." Sonny nodded and took Ellie from Cooper. "I want the rest of it, Sonny. All of it. Despite what you think, you can trust me."

She hesitated a moment, searching his face, and then nodded again. He wasn't sure if she believed him or had simply resigned herself to the task of feeding the baby.

"I'll be right back. Do you mind warming a bottle for me while I change her diaper?"

"I'll get it," Cooper said.

"Thank you."

Gil watched Sonny go to the bedroom in her bare feet. Her wet hair was starting to curl as it dried. He longed to touch those curls, to let her hair spill into his hands. And he hated himself for wanting even that much.

She closed the door behind her without looking back.

"If this isn't really Eduardo Sanchez's baby, why would he appear on television saying that it is?" Marco asked skeptically. "Why be that brazen? I mean, news like this would get picked up by the wire services and be all over the world in minutes."

"No one is going to pay any attention to this kidnapping outside of Colombia," Gil said. "It might be news for a day, but the rest of the world will move on quickly."

Gil glanced at the television screen. He picked up the remote and flipped through several channels. The news was only on one station so far. He went to the window to look at the military trucks. So far, the soldiers were just sitting there. He let the curtain fall back in place.

Gil agreed that Sanchez's actions were bold. Chances were he wouldn't make that kind of move on U.S. soil. But he had so many supporters in Colombia that no one would question him. They'd just rally behind him.

Which didn't bode well for Gil and his team. *Or Sonny and Ellie.*

Marco headed for the kitchen. "Boss man, I'm going to go do some digging."

"That's a good idea. You heard the lady. Dig deep. I need to know exactly who and what we're dealing with. And let me know as soon as you find something."

"Will do."

Gil needed space. Pushing the double doors open to the courtyard, he went outside for some fresh air. It was hot and the sound of commotion in the city altered the space that had been a serene refuge last night when he'd been thinking of Sonny.

Cooper appeared at the French doors but didn't venture outside. "I gave Sonny a bottle for the baby."

He could read her expression. "What's on your mind, Cooper?"

"Not for nothing, Gil, but if this were anyone else, you'd be making plans to fly us out of here."

Floored by her abrupt remark, he said, "What does that mean?"

She rolled her eyes. "Come on, Gil."

Irritation spiked inside him. Not at Cooper, but at himself for being so transparent. If this were anyone else other than Sonny Montgomery, would he be acting any differently?

He didn't like the answers that came to mind.

"What I need you to do right now is help Marco. Will you do that for me?"

Cooper sighed and turned on her heels. He couldn't win this fight, he decided. Mostly because Cooper was right.

For the first time since he started bounty hunting with Bruce, his first partner, he'd gotten in over his head on a job. He knew he needed to do whatever it took to protect his team. He learned that the hard way with Bruce.

The logical thing to do wasn't even an option in Gil's book. Turning Sonny over to the Colombian authorities was unimaginable. And he didn't want to think of what they would do to Sonny if they found her here with Ellie. Yet he had an obligation not to endanger Marco and Cooper.

Gil stayed in the courtyard a few minutes more, letting the warm breeze ease his senses and calm his mind. It was the woman and not the situation that had him so rattled. He knew that, even though he didn't like it very much.

"It's going to take a while to find out what this Eduardo Sanchez is all about," he heard Marco say to Cooper in the kitchen.

Gil decided to go inside. He had to figure out what they were dealing with.

"The press treats him like he's royalty," he heard Marco say. "Cleaning up run-down parts of Colombia and bringing jobs to impoverished villages has practically made the man a local hero."

The door to the bedroom opened and then closed, quietly. Sonny appeared to be considerably calmer at first glance, but Gil's heart nearly broke when he realized she was terrified. Her eyes were red-rimmed and her face was sheet-white. But she kept her shoulders straight and her chin high.

She was prepared to fight and fight hard, Gil realized. He hadn't understood it at the time, but he'd seen that same look at the airport. She hadn't backed down then.

If she was dealing with the kind of trouble he thought she was, he admired her strength. But her stupidity for allowing herself to get involved in something like this in the first place irritated him to no end.

"I got a photo of Eduardo Sanchez and his wife holding their new baby at a press conference," Marco called from the kitchen.

Sonny closed her eyes slowly, shielding her emotion from him.

"It's grainy so it's not going to tell us much about the baby."

Gil continued to look at Sonny, who hadn't moved from where she was standing in the middle of the living room. "What's the date?"

"I'm guessing it will be around three months ago," Sonny said, looking directly at him.

"About three months ago," Marco called out.

Silence hung in the air for a few seconds as Sonny and Gil looked at each other.

Gil finally asked, "Who is really Ellie's mother?"

Sonny shook her head. "How many times are you going to ask me this? My sister-in-law, Serena Davco-Montgomery, is Ellie's biological mother. She gave birth to her at home, so you won't find any birth announcement under that name. You won't even find a wedding announcement about Cash and Serena, so don't even waste your time trying. I'm not sure how much you'll find about Serena's parents except that her mother died in the tragic fire that Manuel Turgis set. You'll find information about the fire, but not about Turgis's involvement—I only learned that myself about two months ago. There won't be much on Serena, if anything at all. Her father, Byron Davco, worked hard to keep her out of the public eye."

"Why?"

"To protect her."

"From Eduardo Sanchez?"

"Among others. I'm not really sure how many people are involved in the deals Byron Davco made to launder money."

"Serena Davco-Montgomery." He said the name as if he were trying it on for size. "Cash's wife."

"Yes."

"Why is there no record of the marriage?"

"That story is going to take a while."

"I've got time. Lots of it."

She shook her head. "You have less time than you realize. Those military trucks you heard outside probably *were* sent by Eduardo Sanchez."

"I figured as much," Gil said. "It's hard to believe a businessman has the power to move the military. Even here in Colombia."

"He's a high-ranking kingpin who wouldn't hesitate to kill any one of us right now if his people found us with Ellie. He's decided she's his. That's all that matters. His wife wanted a baby but couldn't have one. So when the opportunity presented itself, he took Ellie."

"Forgive me if I find this a little farfetched," Gil said. "He couldn't just waltz right into the United States and take a baby, Sonny. And why Ellie?"

"None of this is out of the blue. Taking Ellie was just one way in a long list of ways that Manuel Turgis has tortured this family. Byron Davco made the payments to Manuel Turgis for years, which Turgis in turn used to satisfy Eduardo Sanchez. All that money filtered into these poor hill towns that made Sanchez a local hero. In part, it was Byron Davco's payments along with drug money they laundered."

She sighed and sat down in the empty chair.

"Now that Byron Davco is stricken with Alzheimer's in a nursing home, no payments are being made. The trouble for Cash, Serena and Ellie started when Turgis stopped receiving the protection money."

"What did Turgis do?"

"He planted an informant inside the Davco home. Her name was Susan. She earned Serena's trust and the trust of the staff. All the while, she filtered information back to Turgis to use against the Davco family."

Sonny covered her face with her hands for a moment. When she lifted her gaze to him, he saw the toll the past few weeks had taken on her.

"Go on," he urged.

"Obviously, Manuel Turgis has been working with Eduardo Sanchez for years. Sanchez is the hero around these parts. Turgis does the dirty work."

"Okay, so Sanchez wanted a kid. Why not just adopt legally?"

She laughed humorlessly. "You're not asking the right questions, Gil."

"Then tell me what they are and I'll ask them," he said, his voice booming with frustration. "I have a feeling we don't have time for playing games."

"You're right. And I never intended to. If you recall, I would have been back in the United States twenty-four hours ago if you hadn't stopped me. You went looking for a man who, in your mind, is a criminal. Yet you took an innocent woman and baby and put them in harm's way, just so you could collect your precious bounty."

Sonny practically spat the words at him. Gil could feel her anger as if it were a sledgehammer hitting him square in the face. She'd been desperate to get on that plane. And he'd been determined to stop her at all costs. How big a price had he asked them all to pay?

"There's nothing we can do about that now."

She laughed incredulously. "So Ellie and I are to

pay for it? That's easy for you to live with as long as you collect your money, right?"

He couldn't blame her for thinking that way. But she was dead wrong. However, he wasn't going to get her to believe that now.

"Just tell me what you know about Eduardo Sanchez."

"He's a twisted man. He didn't want just any baby. He wanted Ellie in order to send a message to the Davcos after the protection money stopped."

Marco came charging into the living room. "Gil, buddy, you've got to see this. This is bad."

"I know that."

Marco shook his head quickly. "No, man, I really don't think you do. I tapped into the Aztec Corporation server. Piece of cake. There's nothing there that can't be found on Google. But there's a small private file—"

"Hidden within the corporate mainframe," Sonny finished for him. "But there's a rotating security code that resets the password. You'll have trouble getting in again. You won't be able to use the same steps."

"How do you know?" Marco said.

"Because that's how I found out where Ellie was." At his look of awe, she added, "Don't look so surprised. You know what I do for a living."

"So after you found the file, you came down here to kidnap the baby."

She pleaded with her eyes and it broke his heart. Many criminals had pleaded with him over the years. They all begged him to let them go. But it was Sonny whose tender smile and fiery determination broke him down.

"Gil, Ellie belongs with Serena and..." Sonny seemed to catch herself. "And if it's God's will, then with Cash, too. Regardless of what you believe or what the district attorney believes, Cash didn't skip bail. If he could have been there to prove his innocence, he would have been. He came down here for the same reason I did—to get Ellie."

Gil frowned, unable to comprehend it all. "He had to have been out of his mind to allow such a thing."

"Cash has no idea I'm here."

"And Dylan? Did he willingly put you in this kind of danger?"

Sonny rubbed her temples with her fingers. "He had no choice. I was the only one who could do it. It was too dangerous for my parents, or any of the other family members."

"What about Dylan?"

She hesitated a moment. "He's busy."

Gil's jaw clenched. Unable to stay still, he paced the floor. "Too busy to talk his kid sister out of coming down to Colombia and possibly getting herself killed? Too busy to take the heat for you, to *protect* you?"

She threw her hands up in the air. "Oh, you're a fine one to judge."

"You were already knee-deep in this trouble before I showed up on the scene. All I did was stop you from finishing what you set out to do. You shouldn't even be here. If I loved... If you were my sister, there's no way I would have let you leave the United States and get anywhere near Eduardo Sanchez."

She lifted her chin. "Then it's a good thing I'm not your sister."

They held each other's stare for a moment, locked in a challenge. Gil could look into those dark-blue eyes all day, which was a problem he could no longer ignore. Her fire and tenacity hit him square in the face one moment and brought him to his knees the next. He didn't like admitting it much, but he was deep in his own trouble.

Never in a million years could Gil think of Sonny as a sister. But he almost wished he could. It would make it infinitely easier to think about his next move if he weren't so distracted by her, wanting to pull her into his arms and gaze deep into her eyes every time she looked at him.

Terror began to course through his veins as he thought of all the things that could have happened to Sonny over the past few weeks—and what might happen to her if he didn't think fast.

"I screwed up," he said. "I should have seen this coming."

Instead of thinking about Cash, he'd been thinking of Cash's little sister. He'd had tunnel vision where she was concerned and look where it had gotten them all.

Marco shoved a picture he'd just printed off the computer into Gil's hands.

"Whatever we do, we'd better do it fast. This was in Eduardo Sanchez's private file. He wants Ellie back alive. And whoever finds her is to show no mercy to the person who took her."

Gil glanced down at the picture and felt the earth crumble beneath his feet.

"What is it?" Sonny asked.

He flipped the picture over so Sonny could see and she gasped.

"It's you. At the airport. Holding Ellie."

EIGHT

The morning had started out so well. Sonny had actually gotten out of bed feeling less afraid than she had since learning of the kidnapping. She felt safe, as if all the horrible nightmares she'd been having were just that— nightmares that would vanish as soon as the sun came up.

Boy, what a delusion that was. Nothing had changed. If anything, the nightmare had only gotten worse.

"I won't give this baby over to Eduardo Sanchez."

"I know."

"Gil?" Marco moved closer and lowered his voice, although there was no way for Sonny to avoid hearing him since she was standing right there. "Gil, if they come here we won't have a choice. They're not the kind of people who will say 'pretty please.'"

"Then we'd better hope they don't come here," Gil answered resolutely.

"Too late," Cooper said, looking out the window.

Gil charged toward her. "Why?"

"They're banging on doors." Cooper turned and looked at Sonny. "I'm surprised they are even bothering to knock."

Gil blew out an exasperated breath. "It just gets

better by the minute. Sonny, do you recognize that man talking to the soldiers?"

Sonny came to the window and peered outside into the parking lot.

"Oh, no!" she said in a harsh whisper. "That's Manuel Turgis. I've seen his picture. He'll know who I am."

"Gil, Turgis can't find Sonny here," Cooper said.

Gil looked around the room, at the windows, at the door to the courtyard. "Come in here," he said, advancing toward the bedroom.

Sonny followed. "The hotel knows we have a baby here."

"Cooper and Marco, do something to stall them," Gil said, pushing the bedroom door open.

"Are you kidding?" Marco said. "How do you stall Colombian military?"

"Figure it out, Marco." He pulled Sonny into the bedroom. "Come with me. They know we have a baby with us, but they don't know we have Ellie," Gil added. "If the hotel knew for sure Ellie was the baby the authorities were looking for, the soldiers would have been in here by now. My guess is they're on a hunt. We don't have much time to hide you."

Startled, she stopped short of picking Ellie up from her crib. "What do you mean me? We need to hide Ellie."

Gil turned to her and held her back from taking the baby. "Get in the tub."

"What?"

Sonny heard the pounding on the door to the villa and her blood ran cold. *Lord, what are we going to do?*

"Trust me, Sonny. Get in the tub."

Sonny stared at Ellie in the crib. She was still asleep, even though she was stirring. But in a matter of seconds she'd be wailing from the noise of the soldiers bursting into the room.

"You're going to have to take a leap of faith on this, Sonny," Gil urged, pulling her into the bathroom.

"I can't do it," she whispered, trying to pull out of his grip.

Gil held her tightly by the arm. "Manuel Turgis is out there, and he's looking for you—not just Ellie. Now I can fool him with regard to Ellie, but you are a different story."

She glanced around the room. There was nowhere to hide.

"Get in the tub, pull the curtain and be quiet. I'm going to leave the door open. It'll look less suspicious. Whether you like it or not, you're going to have to trust that I'll take care of Ellie."

"Don't give her to them, Gil. Please." She climbed into the tub, fighting to keep herself together as tears sprang to her eyes.

Crouching down, she felt the moisture from the tub seep through her shirt and onto her skin. She closed her eyes and prayed. *I will lie down and sleep in peace, for You alone, O Lord, make me dwell in safety.* Sonny kept praying, asking the Lord to extend a safety net on all of them.

The door to the bedroom burst open and Sonny jumped, her foot banging against the tub. The urge to bolt from her hiding place was overwhelming. Ellie was in the next room. And so were the soldiers.

She heard Marco and Gil complaining loudly to

someone about the intrusion. She knew the voice talking with them belonged to Manuel Turgis. Sonny tried to stop shaking.

"Where is your wife?" he asked Gil.

"Out shopping. You know women."

There was a short silence, as if he was weighing Gil's answer. The sound of boots on the floor grew louder.

"This baby. Where are the papers?"

"My wife carries them with her. You can't just come in here. What's this all about?" Gil argued.

Sonny closed her eyes, listening to the exchange.

Turgis ignored Gil's question. "How old is the little girl?"

Gil laughed. "I think you need glasses, bud. When was the last time you saw a baby girl wearing Ninja Turtles. My son is four months old."

"Your son?"

"Yes. His name is Charlie."

Sonny could hear Ellie fussing. It sounded as if she was being jiggled up and down. Sonny hated the idea of her being so close to Turgis. But if Gil had Ellie in his arms, she felt certain he'd fight to keep her there.

"The baby doesn't look like a boy."

"Well, at this age, it's hard to tell. But don't say that to my wife. She thinks he looks like me. You still haven't told me what this is all about," Gil said.

"A child has been taken," Turgis said. "We believe she's here in Cartagena."

"Cartagena is a big place."

Sonny heard Turgis advancing toward the bathroom. She sank lower into the tub.

"Charlie here is the only baby in this villa," Gil said,

his voice slightly raised. "I haven't seen any other babies since we've been here."

"Do you have a problem with us searching your room?" Turgis said in a deadly calm voice.

Gil's voice turned matter-of-fact. "I've got nothing to hide. I'm just saying you're wasting your time here if you're looking for a little girl."

There was silence for an agonizing moment. Sonny fought to keep herself still, to silence her breathing and still the trembling that kept rattling the shower curtain.

"I apologize for the disturbance," Turgis finally said, his voice getting quieter as he walked away from the bathroom door.

Sonny felt pain in her hands. Opening her eyes, she saw that her hands were clenched into fists and her fingernails were digging into the soft flesh of her palm.

She was no longer able to hear their voices. They must have moved into the living room. Or maybe her heart was pounding so loudly she couldn't hear anything else. She stayed still, until the shower curtain was yanked open.

A scream rose in her throat and turned to a sob of relief when she saw Gil standing there with Ellie in his arms. She scrambled to her feet, stepped out of the tub and snatched the baby from Gil, bringing her to her chest.

"That was too close," Gil said.

"I never want Ellie near Manuel Turgis again." She kissed Ellie on the cheek, then looked at her pajamas. "I suddenly love Ninja Turtles."

Gil gave her a half grin. "Score one for Cooper."

"I should be the one to go for supplies," Cooper said. Gil dropped the picture of Sonny from the airport on the end table. He couldn't say that he was at ease again after the close encounter of the Colombian-Army-kind earlier. The fear he'd felt earlier when Turgis walked to the bathroom and looked inside was unlike anything he'd ever felt. He was sure Turgis would pull back the curtain to find Sonny there. They'd been lucky.

Gil turned to Cooper. "Well, Sonny certainly can't go and forget Marco."

Marco straightened. "Hey, why not me?"

"Because babies don't have computer components and you wouldn't know what to look for," Cooper said.

With a roll of his eyes, Marco said, "You bought boy clothes for the baby."

"Those *boy* clothes saved our skins, in case you have forgotten."

"What happens when we leave the villa?" Sonny asked. "We can't stay here forever."

Cooper nodded. "She's right. Forget the supplies. Let's get on a plane now and get out of here, Gil. We'll go looking for Cash again once things settle down. Sitting in a hot spot here in Colombia isn't doing us any good."

There'd be other bounties, other criminals to bring to justice. But none of that was on Gil's mind. Right now, keeping Sonny, the baby and his team alive was what mattered.

The fact that there was a photo of Sonny with Ellie at the airport was huge. It changed everything. Gil knew they needed a new plan.

"Sonny and Ellie can't leave by air," Gil said. He dropped down to the sofa. "We're going to need to think of another way."

"Just because Sanchez has an airport photo of her

and the baby doesn't mean that every airport in Colombia will be circulating it," Cooper said.

Sonny sighed. "Timing was critical. The only reason I dared to use the papers I have was because I was sure Sanchez wouldn't have enough time to come after me before I boarded the plane. Once I'd left the country with Ellie, we'd be on U.S. soil and protected by the U.S. government."

"What about the American Embassy?" Marco asked.

Sonny groaned. "The embassy in Bogotá couldn't really help us. They said we could go there, but we'd have to remain there and it would be risky to leave."

"Who exactly is *we?*"

Sonny bit her lip, recalling the image of Lucia slumped over in the backseat.

"I was working with some people here in Colombia. Ellie didn't have a passport when I came here. Eduardo Sanchez must have been able to bypass these legalities because not having a passport or birth certificate didn't seem to be a problem for him. He was able to get her into the country and even establish that she was 'legally' adopted. I doubt anyone here was really interested in challenging him, anyway.

"Serena applied for a passport in the United States using an old picture she had of Ellie and a birth certificate she had drawn up after Ellie was taken. She explained it had been a home birth, so they gave it to her after the fact. The paperwork was going to take some time. As soon as it came through, I applied for a duplicate from the embassy in Bogotá and asked them for help. They supplied the duplicate and were good enough to push it through quickly."

"Did they know about Ellie being taken?" Gil asked.

"No. I asked around at the embassy when I applied for the duplicate passport about safe places for American citizens, but I didn't say why. They said the only safe place for us was inside the embassy, but that anything I did I'd be doing on my own, without official American help.

"I was afraid to be discovered. I could walk the streets, but I couldn't go near Sanchez's estate. If Sanchez's people knew I was here, I would have disappeared."

Sonny didn't have to elaborate on that further. Gil had a pretty good idea of what men like Manuel Turgis and Eduardo Sanchez could do.

Sonny turned to Marco. "Did the file contain my name?"

Marco shook his head. "Just the picture."

"It won't take them long to figure out who I am. And if Sanchez realizes I'm Cash's sister, I won't be able to get on a plane using my passport."

Gil thought a minute. "What about Ellie?"

"No."

"Why not?" Cooper asked. "Why can't I take her back to the U.S.? We could split you two up."

Sonny turned to Cooper. "I appreciate your trying to help. But it's not possible."

"You think I'll hand her over?"

Sonny shook her head. "No, Cooper, I don't. But you can't travel with her unless you have permission from her mother. And that permission needs to be verified and notarized. It's required in America because there are too many child kidnappings by parents who are natural citizens of other countries. Once the child is physically in the other country, that country's custody laws take precedence, making it difficult for the United States to intercede."

"How did you plan on getting her back to the U.S.?" Marco asked.

"I have her birth certificate, her passport and notarized permission from her mother. Without all three, she can't board a plane. And now that Eduardo Sanchez has made his quest public, every airport in Colombia will be on the lookout for a baby traveling without their parents." She looked at all of them. "If I can get into the United States, we'll be safe. It's leaving Colombia that's the problem."

Gil nodded.

"I hate to be the bearer of bad news but we're a long way from the United States," Marco said, tapping a pencil on his hand in a staccato motion.

Gil stood up and walked to the French doors leading to the courtyard. "Not so far that we can't make it."

"You've got a plan, boss?" Marco said with a gleam in his eye.

He turned to Sonny. "Possibly. Any way we can get in touch with your brother Dylan?"

Sonny felt disappointment wash over her. For a brief moment, she thought perhaps Gil had come up with a way to get them safely out of Colombia. But any plan involving Dylan wouldn't work.

"Truthfully, any other time, Dylan would be the first person I'd call. But I don't know where he is."

Gil eyed her skeptically.

"I'm telling you the truth, Gil. They purposely didn't tell me what they were doing to protect me and Cash."

"He knows where Cash is, though."

"Seems we might have been tailing the wrong sibling," Marco said.

Sonny glared at Marco. "When I cracked the private file in the Aztec Corporation's computer system, I found information about Cash being held in a prison here in Colombia. It didn't say where. But I'm hoping Dylan was able to find it." She looked directly at Gil. "If Cash has any chance of getting out of that prison alive, you can't interfere with what Dylan's doing. They could all be killed if you get in the way."

And then she would have lost both of her brothers. *Lord, losing Dylan and Cash is unthinkable to me.*

"We've got bigger problems to deal with right now," he said with regret. "Besides, I won't make that same mistake of getting in your way twice."

The relief Sonny felt was overwhelming. "Okay, how are we going to get out of Colombia?"

He stared out at the courtyard for a minute. "Let's backtrack. How did you know where to find Ellie?"

"I didn't. I only knew Eduardo Sanchez had an adopted baby from America. Lucia was the one who found her."

"Lucia? Is that the person you were working with?" Marco asked. "How many people are involved with this?"

"She's part of a child rescue organization. Dylan knew her briefly during his years in the military." She paused a moment, overwhelmed by the memory of seeing Lucia in the backseat. "She retired from the military a few years before Dylan did and used her training to help rescue kidnapped children."

"Was she the one who actually took Ellie from Sanchez's estate?"

"Yes."

"It seems odd she didn't accompany you to the airport to make sure you got on the plane." Gil paced in front of her. "If she worked in any kind of Special Forces capacity with your brother she would've known how to stop me from interfering with you."

Sonny's eyes filled with tears. "At least she got Ellie out of Sanchez's house."

"How'd she do it?"

"She got a job as a housekeeper at the estate. She got to know the routine of all the guards and Ellie's nanny. I didn't know until the night before exactly what the plan was and when I was going to be leaving. I don't even know the details of how Lucia actually got Ellie out of the estate. And truthfully, I'm not sure I want to know—they were both in serious danger."

"So you just hung around the hotel room and waited for someone to call you?" Cooper asked.

Sonny shook her head. "No phones. Torres—he was another member of the organization—had a contact in the marketplace. I would go down there to buy food and if there was news, he would give it to me. I spent a lot of days in that hotel room wondering what was going on."

Marco blew out a quick breath. "Must have been torture."

"Lucia would come to the marketplace and meet me, too. She didn't relay much information. It was mostly to update me on Ellie's condition at the estate."

"And then she left you holding the bag at the airport,"

Cooper said, with a disapproving shake of her head. "That's no way to work as a team."

"Lucia was killed the morning she took Ellie. She was already dead by the time Torres brought Ellie to me."

Her father, Sonny thought. She closed her eyes and said a prayer for Torres, for the hard journey he had to make in telling Lucia's husband and young son that she had been killed. The man who'd helped bring Cash and Serena's baby back to her family was now grieving for his own child.

"What happened? Who killed her? Eduardo? One of his guards?"

"I don't know. Her…" She was about to say "her father," but it was too awful to say out loud. "Torres was very vague. I was supposed to meet them in the marketplace very early that morning. They didn't want to risk going back to the hotel to get me."

"I lost you that morning," Gil said. "It was only after Marco checked the airport records that I discovered you'd confirmed a flight to leave that day. That was hours later."

"I didn't want to leave from Bogotá. And Lucia thought it was best that I leave from a popular airport where there was room for me to get lost among the tourists."

Gil smiled weakly. "She was right. I had a hard time finding you. I finally gave up and waited for you at airport security."

"Lucia was supposed to come back with me to Miami. But when I got in the car, she was dead. Torres told me it had nothing to do with taking Ellie from the Sanchez estate. He said that an old debt had been repaid.

I'm not sure I believe him, though. The last thing he said to me was to make sure that I got Ellie out of Colombia. Once I got out of the car, I knew he couldn't help me anymore."

Gil looked at her for a long time. Sonny wasn't sure what he was thinking. His expression was unreadable.

"Marco doesn't have to waste any more time looking for the e-mail I sent," Sonny said.

Gil smirked. "No, he doesn't. Because he already found it."

A slight smile of admiration played on her lips. "And here I thought I was being good."

"You were," Marco said, waggling his eyebrows. "It took a while, but I'm relentless."

"The e-mail didn't say much," Gil said. "Care to elaborate?"

"I needed to tell my father that I wasn't on the plane, but that I had Ellie and we were alive."

Cooper stood up. "How did you expect to get into the United States with a baby that didn't have an entry stamp on her passport? Wouldn't they have detained you?"

"Possibly. But being on U.S. soil at that point would have made all the difference. They could have held me in immigration as long as they wanted. I had her birth certificate, and Serena was meeting me at the gate with the original passport. Eventually it would have been straightened out."

"Well, a quick plane ride sounds good to me." Cooper put up her hands and let them fall down by her side. "What do you say, boss man? Do we find a different airport and get out of here?"

Sonny looked up at Cooper, and then at Gil. He was silent for a moment.

"I'd say you and Marco need to pack up your gear and get on a plane to the States as soon as possible. This hot spot doesn't look like it's going to cool down any time soon."

Marco looked at him with surprise. "And split the team? No can do."

Cooper jumped up from the chair. "No way. No one gets left behind. We're a team, Gil."

And they were a tight team at that, Sonny realized. Their loyalty to each other was evident. She was the one standing in the way of their safety. Cooper had made that very clear.

"I think Gil is right," she said. "You all need to get out of Colombia quickly. Your association with me is only going to make trouble for you." She turned to Gil. The worried look etched on his rugged features only added to his appeal. "You, too, Gil," she said, tears stinging the back of her eyes. The thought that he'd leave her now terrified her, but being the cause of another person's death was something she simply couldn't live with.

His eyes flew open and then his expression turned hard. "Are you crazy? You'll never get out of Colombia alive on your own."

"Gil, no bounty is worth your life," she argued. "You should go back to the States."

"Forget the bounty. I'm not going to leave you here to fend for yourself. How far do you think you'll get with a baby in tow and soldiers crawling the streets?"

"There's got to be a way, Gil. Some other way," Cooper said.

A cry from the bedroom pulled Sonny's attention away from the conversation.

Cooper stilled her with her hand. "I'll take care of her. You figure something out."

She thought about it. "I don't know. I honestly don't know what to do. If Dylan were here—"

"You already said Dylan can't help you. I can, and I'm right here. I'm not leaving you."

Emotion clogged her throat. She couldn't go through this alone anymore—and Gil was saying she didn't have to. "Please. Let me use your computer to get in touch with my father."

Marco looked at both of them. "I don't get it. Chances are, Dylan is here, right? Why not get his help? He must have already figured out a plan to get out of Colombia. He probably has a whole team with him."

She shook her head. "I have no way to get in touch with Dylan. I'm not even sure my father knows where he is right now."

Gil looked at Sonny directly. "I'm going to get you out of Colombia, Sonny. I promised you at the airport that I would get you back to the United States. And I mean to do that."

Tears filled her eyes. "Technically, you didn't promise anything. You never answered me."

"Well, I'm answering now. We just have to get you home without going by air."

"We can drive north, maybe take a plane from Panama City. I could find us a route." Marco turned to go to the kitchen, but Gil stopped him.

"Do you really think Sanchez won't be able to track us there?" Gil asked. "We'll still have to contend with the borders. They're going to check passports. It's too risky. I've already jeopardized your lives enough."

Sonny looked at Gil with surprise. "You? You can't blame yourself for what's happening now."

The dark eyes that had intrigued her were full of regret. "I should have let you get on that plane."

Yes, he should have. But they couldn't turn back the clock. "Things would be a lot easier right now if you had," she said quietly. "But you can't blame yourself."

"This is my team. I not only put their lives in danger, but now I've put yours—and Ellie's—in danger, as well. It was my call."

"But not your fault. Look, I've spent these last few months wondering how this became my life. My family has been caught in one tangled web after another. I've seen how people lay blame without really knowing the truth. Don't do that to yourself. It only ends up making matters worse."

"I appreciate what you're saying but—"

"You can't stay here, Gil," Cooper said, breaking into the conversation. She had the baby in her arms. Ellie was awake, smiling and gumming her fist, completely unaware of the turmoil around her.

With a resolute sigh, he said, "I'm not going to. None of us are. You and Marco are going to leave today. There's nothing tying you to Sonny and the baby. There's no reason for you not to get on the plane at the airport without any hassle."

"And you?" Marco said. "What are you going to do?"

He thought a minute, and then stood.

"Right now, I'm going to take a walk. I need to clear my head. I don't want to be running scared only to find out there was nothing to run from. All we have right now is speculation."

"And that picture," Sonny said.

He nodded. "And the picture. In the meantime, hold off on contacting your father until we have a definite plan. No sense risking an intercept when we don't have anything concrete to report."

"I have to contact him at some point. He's going to worry. All he knows is that I have Ellie. But by now he's probably frantic not knowing what's going on."

Gil nodded and headed for the door.

"Where are you going?" Sonny asked.

"Shopping."

Without another word, Gil walked out the door.

NINE

The streets of Cartagena were humming in a way that didn't bring to mind jovial music and laughter. A frenetic fear was in the air. Vendors who would normally accost you on the street to make a sale were a little more hesitant with all the military trucks rolling down the streets of the marketplace.

Gil walked by a grand structure with brightly colored tiles adorning the outside and elegant archways framing the first story, shielding the porch from the hot Colombian sun. Woven baskets were stacked high against the inside of the porch, one on top of the other. The second floor balconies were beautifully decorated with colorful potted plants that trailed over the railing, almost down to the first floor.

Vendors hurried to put their items for sale on their carts. Every so often, a military vehicle would roll down the center of the street, commanding their attention. The vendors stood for a fraction of a moment and stared, wondering who had caused such a disturbance in their otherwise routine lives.

Gil walked past them without looking. If they only

knew all this fuss was for a little baby who never should have been in Colombia in the first place.

People were nervous. He could feel it like the pulse in his hand. Even if people hadn't heard about Eduardo Sanchez's press conference or didn't care, they knew something was up.

In a country where the law was a blurred line that was easily crossed, people turned inward as a matter of survival. They knew the dust would settle eventually. But it usually involved bloodshed and someone's disappearance.

Right now, the quaint balconies that the locals sat on in the early morning before the heat became unbearable were empty except for the flowers in their pots. People laughed and bartered and went on with their daily lives, but every so often he could see them scanning the streets, as if searching for the source of unrest.

Gil didn't know where he was going. He just walked. As he reached the old military dungeons that had been transformed into quaint shops, he realized he never should have brought his team to Colombia. No matter how quick Sonny was to let him off the hook, Gil knew he'd put his team in danger. She hadn't judged him but it didn't matter. He didn't have a harsher critic than himself.

That speech Sonny had given him about not blaming himself had to do with her brother Cash. Gil was sure of it. Had people blamed him unjustly? Was there more to his story than anyone was giving credence to?

It happened all the time, as he well knew. People's lives could easily be destroyed by false accusations and a rush to judgment. It wasn't his place to judge Cash

Montgomery or his sister. But he had anyway, he realized.

Gil had always been of the belief that if you didn't have something to hide, then you let justice take its course. Only guilty people ran. That's what his first partner, Bruce, had always said.

That was a joke, he thought, wiping the sweat off his forehead with the back of his hand. Guilty people didn't always run. And sometimes, the people who loved them intervened with deadly force out of revenge or fear. That's what had happened to his partner, Bruce. They hadn't underestimated the danger of the fugitive they were trying to apprehend, but they had underestimated his wife, who put a bullet in Bruce's head. Now Bruce's wife was a widow.

Bruce and Karen had been married only two years. But it seemed like so much longer. She'd wanted Bruce to get out of bounty hunting so they could start a family. He'd wanted his last bounty to be a big one and it cost him his life. That's it, *adios amigo.*

The last time Gil had seen Karen, she'd said she was happy. She was married again to a cop who already had two children from a previous marriage. But when she looked at her new husband, Gil couldn't see that sparkle in her eye she'd always had when she'd looked at Bruce. And when Bruce had looked at her.

Only guilty people run. Well, not in Bruce's case. Justice hadn't prevailed and no one was doing time in the state penitentiary for killing him. *I'm not going to take the chance of losing another partner just for a bounty.*

How Sonny could so easily let him off the hook for

putting her life in further danger was beyond him. But then, the woman was a tough one to figure out. She had determination, guts—not every woman would go head-to-head in a hot zone with a kingpin like Eduardo Sanchez. Gil actually didn't know if that amounted to bravery or insanity.

And Sonny had faith. He couldn't help but wonder if leaving his faith behind had been where he'd taken the wrong road in his life.

He continued to walk for a while, listening to the chatter of the people but not really taking it in. He came to the brick footpath leading to Castillo de San Felipe de Barajas, one of the many fortresses built on the coast of Cartagena to protect the city from pirates in the sixteenth century. From the top of the fortress, he could see the whole city and the Caribbean Sea. It was strange, he thought, that the walls could protect the city from those outside it, but not from those inside—like Eduardo Sanchez.

Colombia adored Eduardo Sanchez. The people here would go to great lengths to thank him for the work he'd done, including putting military soldiers on the Aztec Corporation payroll. Heads were turned when the right amount of money was flashed in front of them.

Marco had found good information about Eduardo Sanchez and the Aztec Corporation. But what Sonny knew would help them move in the right direction more quickly.

Gil made his way back toward the square and stopped at a cart to look at some brightly woven cloth the vendor was selling. Just then, a military truck passed him, slowing to a stop. Gil saw four soldiers in the back, their guns trained on the crowd of people in the square.

They were definitely looking for something or someone. But Gil couldn't allow paranoia to make him think it was Ellie.

He dropped the fabric back on the cart, much to the protest of the vendor, who continued to yell after him as Gil walked away.

The soldiers jumped off the back of the truck and walked through the square, stopping tourists with small children, talking to street vendors. With a shake of their heads, the soldiers moved on. The relief in the tourists' faces was evident.

The cathedral, one of Cartagena's grandest structures that could be seen from anywhere in the city, was just a few hundred feet away. There were many beautiful old churches in Cartagena, some as old as the city itself. But the elegant cathedral, with its high spire and ornate design, was the grand dame of them all. It seemed to beckon Gil to come inside.

Gil looked up at the stone face and wondered why he'd ended up here. He hadn't sought out the company of the Lord in many years. But then, he'd found many surprises on this trip. He surprised himself once more by climbing the stone steps, pulling on the brass door handle and walking inside.

Gil found an empty bench and did something he hadn't done in many years. He bent his head, and he prayed.

"Why is he being so hard on himself?" Sonny asked Cooper as she burped the baby over her shoulder. "This isn't his fault. Well, not completely."

Cooper rolled her eyes. "It's a character flaw. He has this thing about being the mighty man. He never got over his childhood dream of being a superhero."

Sonny chuckled, and was surprised that even with the sound of commotion on the streets outside the courtyard she was still able to laugh. But Cooper didn't laugh. The faraway look in her eyes told Sonny that she was worried. She wasn't the only one.

"I get the feeling he's very protective of you, too," Sonny said.

Cooper shrugged, then picked at a colorful flower by the stone bench she was sitting on. "He claims it's part of his charm but I find it totally annoying. He thinks he needs to protect everyone."

"Why?"

She blew out a quick breath. "He'd kill me if I told you."

Curious, Sonny settled Ellie on her lap and gave her a rattle to play with. "So don't tell him you told me."

Cooper gave a quick laugh. "Did he tell you he used to be in Special Forces?"

She shook her head. "It doesn't surprise me, though."

"Why?"

"He reminds me of my brother Dylan. Code of honor and all that."

"Like I said, annoying," Cooper sputtered.

"Oh, I don't know about that."

"Years ago, Gil lost a member of his team in a raid while trying to apprehend a fugitive," Cooper explained.

Sonny gasped. "That must have been awful."

"I never met the man. It was before I joined on. But the guy tried to play hero by breaking up a fight. See, the wife of the criminal he was trying to find didn't know the guy was on the run. I guess it was common for him to do this vanishing act every now and then, and she'd just accepted it as part of their marriage."

Sonny made a face. "Strange."

"Yeah, I know. Anyway, the rent was due, the thug didn't have it and wifey had a fit. In comes Gil and his partner, Captain Courageous—I think his name was Bruce—looking to collect their fugitive, right in the middle of the fight."

"What happened?"

"Gil sent the wife in the other room while they put the cuffs on the husband. Gil thought it was odd he didn't try to run. Most fugitives run when they see us coming. It was just long enough for her to go into the bedroom and get a gun."

"He didn't see the gun?"

"Gil? No. But Bruce did. That's when he decided to be a hero and step in front of a bullet to protect his fugitive. The dirtbag fugitive. He didn't want to lose that bounty."

"Wow."

"Yeah, things don't get much heavier than that."

"And Gil feels responsible?"

Cooper threw her hands up in the air and pasted on a mock smile. "He's big brother to all."

"I can see why it would affect Gil, but he can't blame himself for that. He didn't know."

"You don't know Gil like I do. He feels responsible."

"He didn't shoot his partner."

Cooper shook her head. "Doesn't matter. It was his call to go into the house in the first place. Bruce wanted to wait until the suspect came out. His call, his responsibility. Gil doesn't see it any other way."

"Like at the airport."

She shrugged. "Right. The worst part was when it went to trial, the wife got off because she said she thought Gil and Bruce were burglars coming to rob the place."

"And the jury believed that?"

"Yeah. No justice."

Sonny knew there was a whole lot of difference between what had happened to Gil's partner and what was happening now. But she doubted Gil saw it that way.

His call, his responsibility.

"I need to change Ellie's diaper," Sonny said, getting up from the bench. She went into the bedroom, grabbed a towel and placed it on the bed. The baby didn't seem content to stay still on the towel and tried to roll over onto her side with all her might. With one hand on Ellie's stomach to still her, Sonny fished through the suitcase on the floor for a fresh diaper.

"Not for nothing, Sonny," Cooper said, coming into the room, "but Gil doesn't need another distraction, if you know what I mean."

Sonny looked up sharply, her hand still on the baby. "No, I don't know what you mean."

She looked at Sonny for a long moment and then shook her head. "Forget it."

"I can't forget it," Sonny said. "It's out there. What do you mean?"

Cooper rolled her eyes. "Come on, Sonny. You don't see the way he looks at you?"

Heat crept up her cheeks. "He looks at me like he's angry all the time. Yeah, I see that."

Cooper's mouth dropped open. "Fine. Okay, forget I said anything. I thought maybe you could read men a little better than that." She grabbed her empty suitcase and shoved it on the bed. She tossed the clothes she'd had in the bureau drawers into it and zipped it shut before looking at Sonny again.

As she placed the packed suitcase on the floor, she added, "A woman knows when a man looks at her if he means her harm…or if he's in love. But hey, it's none of my business, you know?"

"Is that a warning?"

"Only if you're looking to protect yourself. I've never seen him like this. You've got him all stirred up and that's scary. He's always been the one in control."

Sonny couldn't find the words to answer and instead watched Cooper walk out of the bedroom, leaving her suitcase on the unmade bed. Maid service hadn't been by because they'd put the "Do Not Disturb" sign on the door. They didn't want anyone poking around inside the villa.

Sonny closed her eyes. She wasn't a stupid woman and she knew Gil didn't mean her any harm, regardless of how much they argued over their situation. She had seen something in his eyes last night as they talked and then again this morning before he left for his walk.

Sonny could no longer deny she had a strong attraction to Gil. Especially since it was obvious from Cooper's comment that whatever it was they were feeling was clear to the others.

It had been easy to push aside her feelings at first.

Gil wanted information about Cash, and she couldn't give it to him. She wouldn't have given it to him even if she could. But he'd stopped asking, and something had shifted between them. And now Sonny had no idea how to deal with her fear that she was falling in love with Gil. No idea at all.

TEN

After all these years, Sonny finally understood what it was like for her parents to wait for her to come home after a night out with her friends. No, this was worse, she decided. Much worse. Her parents hadn't had to worry about Eduardo Sanchez and the Aztec Corporation. There was no amount of trouble Sonny could have ever gotten into as a teenager that would compare to this.

Gil wasn't back yet. He'd been gone for hours. Not knowing where he was or what was happening was killing her.

She hated the fact that although she sat in the living room playing with Ellie on the blanket, her attention was focused on the door.

And the man who isn't walking through that door.

Cooper was slouched in a chair with her legs swung over the arm, watching the news. She didn't have to say it, but she was pretty freaked out. She should be. If Gil didn't come back, they'd have to find a way to get out of Colombia without him.

No, she'd have to find a way. Cooper and Marco would be able to walk out of Colombia without anybody watching them. Sonny wanted to say that to Cooper, to ease her anxiety. But something told her that although Gil's team was seriously worried about what they'd been caught in, neither Cooper nor Marco was willing to leave Cartagena without Gil.

Marco had been on the computer all day. She was desperate to e-mail her father. Her parents had to be frantic by now. All three of their children were in Colombia and in danger.

"Is Gil back yet?" Marco said. Sonny had heard the printer whizzing earlier and now Marco held a stack of papers in his hand.

"Hasn't shown his face yet." Cooper turned off the TV and got to her feet. "I'm all ears. What do you have, Marco?"

"Don't you think we should wait—" Sonny never finished her sentence as the door to the villa opened and Gil stepped inside.

"Perfect timing," Marco said. "What's the word on the street?"

Gil dropped a package on the end table and motioned to Sonny with his head. "More supplies for the baby. It should last us a week or so."

She felt disappointment flooding her heart. "That long?"

"I'm afraid so."

"You got something in the works, Gil?" Marco said, pressing him for an answer.

"No one is saying anything on the streets."

Cooper let out a sigh of relief.

"But that doesn't mean anything," Gil added. "It just means they're scared."

"You said no one is saying anything," Cooper said.

"That means we should get out of here while we still can."

"It's not that easy and you know it," Gil said, looking at her with sympathy.

Sonny closed her eyes. When she opened them again Gil was looking at her intently. "Just because people on the streets aren't willing to divulge information about Eduardo Sanchez doesn't mean they don't know what's going on," Sonny said.

"That's right. To anyone here, we're just tourists. Worse, we're Americans. They don't trust us," Gil replied.

"That's what Lucia said, too." Sonny's stomach filled with dread. "She also said that any one of them would give us up in a heartbeat."

Marco looked at all of them. "Well, we can't sit around and do nothing. It's just a matter of time before somebody hears the baby cry and realizes no one has ever laid eyes on her."

"Don't worry. We're going to make our move," Gil said. "Just not tonight."

Gil's eyes met Sonny's for a brief moment and then moved away. There was no plan. At least, nothing set in stone. It amazed Sonny how much she could read Gil—she'd only just met him.

"I need to get in touch with my father, Gil," she said quietly. "I hate that my family doesn't know what's happened to me."

"I understand. But I still think we should wait until we have a concrete plan."

Heaving a sigh, she picked up the baby. Ellie's eyelids were closing. Sonny hardly knew her little niece, making it difficult to know when it was time to put her down for a nap. But it looked like now might be the perfect time.

"I'll be back in a minute," she said, needing a moment for herself. She knew she was going to have to decide whether to stick with Gil or cut both herself and Ellie free so the others had a chance. She just had no clue how to make that decision.

Orange and crimson streaked the sky as if an artist had taken a wide paintbrush and spread color to signal the night was on its way. Gil stood out in the courtyard, looking at the spectacle of color. He'd always liked the peacefulness of dusk, a time of quiet reflection at the end of each day to regroup. But tonight there was a hum inside of him that was growing so strong he was about to jump out of his skin. He doubted anything could quiet it.

Cartagena wasn't known for cool breezes like the kind he remembered from his childhood in Maine. The air off the chilly Atlantic waters had always cooled him in the evening, even on the hottest summer days.

Closing his eyes, he let the warm breeze wash over him. "Lord, please watch over this house, keep everyone within these walls safe in Your hands and deliver us back home without harm," he whispered in prayer.

When he opened his eyes, he was startled to find someone standing below the arch by the French door. Darkness had fallen.

"Talking to the moon? Or just to yourself?"

The smooth voice startled him and his pulse beat faster. But not because of surprise. Gil had come out to the courtyard in the hopes of getting some distance from Sonny. From whatever it was that was making his head spin when he looked in her direction.

He turned and saw how her eyes reflected the bright light of the moon. It was no use. He'd have to go halfway across the world to get enough distance from Sonny—and even that wouldn't be enough. He'd never been so drawn to any woman in his life and now was the absolute wrong time for it to happen.

"Just working through some things in my head," he said, unable to tear his gaze from her.

"I didn't mean to intrude."

"You're not."

She was beautiful, not just pretty like he'd thought earlier. Her dark hair was like midnight with golden streaks of light that made him want to sift his fingers through the strands.

"I came out here earlier with Ellie. I was showing her the flowers in the urns and telling her about colors." Sonny laughed and it sounded musical to Gil's ears. "She didn't have a clue what I was saying, of course, but she still looked at me as if she were hanging on every word."

"She probably was mesmerized by your voice." He knew he was. Sonny's voice was rich and honey-toned. Her mouth stretched into a smile that made her lips all the more appealing.

"Where is the baby now?"

"Cooper is playing with her."

"I'm surprised you let Ellie out of your sight."

"I wanted to talk to you. It's kind of crowded in there with the team," she said. "Don't get me wrong. They've been great."

"They wouldn't treat you wrong, Sonny. No matter what happens. They're just a bit edgy."

"As we all are."

"We're a little far from home in more ways than one."

Even with the benefit of a nearly full moon, he couldn't see her face fully. But he could make out the furrow of her brow, so he explained.

"As bounty hunters, we have a certain amount of latitude as far as the law is concerned in the United States. We're allowed to obtain information and go to certain lengths to apprehend criminals. For example, we don't need to wait for warrants to enter a fugitive's home."

"But not outside U.S. borders?"

He gave her a half smile. "One more thing for you to be angry with me about."

"I'm not angry with you."

You should be. If not for me, you'd be safe right now. So would Ellie, and Marco and Cooper.

"I was angry with you for keeping me from leaving Colombia," Sonny said. "But I know anger isn't going to make this better for us. It's just wasted energy. You had no way of knowing what kind of people are after my family. Sometimes I still can't believe it myself."

Her bottom lip quivered and her eyes glistened with unshed tears.

"The longer we stay here, Sonny, the harder it's going to be for us to leave."

"I know."

When he didn't say more, she groaned and said,

"Come on, Gil. You can jump in at any moment here and play the big hero. You know, tell me that everything is going to be okay and all that."

"Is that what you want? A big hero?"

Her shoulders rose and fell with her sigh. "No, I guess I don't."

"The world is full of big heroes. Not as appealing as they once were, huh?"

"Not if they're not real."

He wasn't going to be a hero to anyone if he couldn't get her and Ellie out of Colombia.

"Cooper and Marco say they're not leaving here without you."

He looked up at the sky, away from her probing stare. "I know."

"I think that's a mistake."

"So do I. But it's hard to break up a team that's been together for as long as we have."

"Cooper said she wasn't with you when you worked with Bruce," Sonny said gently.

He snapped his head toward her.

"She told me about him today," she said, answering his surprise. "It's not the same thing, Gil."

Sonny was still leaning against the column that held up the overhang by the door. Part of him hoped she stayed there. He was honestly afraid of what he'd do if she came any closer.

"Cooper worries too much."

She took a step into the moonlight and it danced on her hair and illuminated her face. Just looking at her took Gil's breath away.

"I don't know about that," she said quietly. "You're

a protector. You may hunt criminals, but you still feel responsible for protecting others."

"Is that right?"

With a roll of her eyes, she laughed. "Go ahead and play the he-man."

Gil chuckled and pinched the bridge of his nose, trying to hide his expression from her. She had him pegged, and he didn't know how much closer she could get before he stopped breathing altogether.

He wanted her to sit with him on the bench, feel her next to him, and yet he didn't invite her. He didn't trust himself not to touch her. Kiss her. He worked to focus on the issue at hand.

"I talked to a man down at the market today who's from Sweden. He was talking to one of the vendors about a job because he's running low on cash. This man—Olof—is sailing alone."

She raised an eyebrow. "What does this have to do with us?"

"We could leave Colombia by boat safer than any other way. I talked to him about taking us to Puerto Rico. He's interested because he needs the cash, but he'll only take us halfway."

Her eyes widened, letting in more light from the moon and making it harder for him to focus on what he was saying.

"Can't he just take us all the way to Puerto Rico? That's U.S. territory. It's as good as Miami."

Gil shook his head and dragged his gaze away from her. "He had a run-in with another sailor on his way down. Seems the Coast Guard got involved and he'd just as soon stay clear."

"What kind of run-in?"

"I didn't ask. And let's be honest. It doesn't really matter as long as he's not a drug runner."

"Do you think he is?"

He shrugged. "We don't have a lot of options. The less said, the better. The important fact about him is he's not Colombian."

"And he doesn't have ties or loyalties to Eduardo Sanchez or his people in any way." Her voice held just a hint of fear. She wouldn't be human if she weren't scared, but it amazed him that most of the time she kept that emotion in check.

"Right."

She looked up at the sky. The breeze was blowing her hair around her face. "When do we leave?"

"Tomorrow, after the money I sent for gets wired— there's a Western Union down at the center of the marketplace. I have to pay Olof up front."

"I don't have money to pay for this. I mean, I can get it. I can have my father wire it."

What Olof was asking for in the way of payment was a small fortune, even for a charter service. But they weren't in a position to bargain for a lower price, so Gil took what he could get and thanked the Lord for the open window He'd provided.

"That won't be necessary. It's taken care of."

"By who?"

"It doesn't matter. The point is I don't want to risk anything coming in that can be traced to you. It's safer that way."

"As safe as it can be," she whispered, glancing down at her hands in her lap.

"Right."

The gentle breeze kicked up her hair again, making it dance for a moment. Then the strands fell back to Sonny's shoulders.

"What are you thinking?" he asked.

She turned to him and their eyes met, locking together as if in a warm embrace. He closed his, to break the connection. It was too powerful for him to handle. And when he opened them again he focused on the curve of Sonny's cheek, on the slight tip of her nose.

Gil wished with all his heart there was some way he could break free of the overwhelming emotions that were cascading down upon him. How could he protect her if he couldn't even think when he was near her?

Sonny said nothing. Instead, she looked right back at him, a storm raging in her dark-blue eyes. A storm Gil wanted to be caught in.

"I want to kiss you," he finally said, his voice just a hair above a whisper.

"I know."

Gil swallowed hard. The distance between them was only a few strides. She gave no invitation, though, so he stayed where he was.

"I can't feel this way about you. It's not right."

She shook her head. "Who's to say what's right and what's wrong? Only God has that authority. And to be honest, I've spent the better part of today trying to figure out how I can be so drawn to the one man who jeopardized my chance of getting out of this country."

Gil dropped his head into his hands. Sonny paced back and forth twice before stopping with her back to him.

"You're right. I should hate you. But I don't."

"I can't imagine why you don't."

Sonny laughed harshly. "This is crazy. I didn't spend today thinking about how I was going to get back home. I spent it waiting for you to come back to the villa. Waiting to see you again."

When she turned to him he saw tears in her eyes. He was still processing the fact that he hadn't been alone in his feelings. Sonny had been battling the same war he felt tearing him up inside. He could now see it in her eyes as clearly as if the sun were shining on them instead of the moon.

A tear trickled down her cheek. "What I really want…" She cleared her throat. "Is to kiss you. Again. For real." Then she drew a deep breath and waited.

And he thought he'd die.

With two wide strides he was by her side. There was nothing he wanted more than to have Sonny in his arms. He reached up and cupped her cheek with his hand, brushing his thumb against a trembling lip, tracing the wetness her tears had left on her cheek.

"This *is* crazy," he whispered. She was in his arms, where he'd dreamed she'd be all along. He bent his head and brushed his lips against hers, holding her, loving her. Crazy or not, nothing could stop him.

And he knew there was no going back.

"We're good to go," Cooper said. "Are you sure you want to do it this way, Gil?"

Gil stuffed the rest of the baby supplies in his suitcase. "It's all set."

Marco had packed up all his computer gear and they'd mapped out a plan that seemed workable. Sonny was too cautious to call it a good plan. They'd had a good plan for getting Ellie out of Eduardo Sanchez's estate and yet Lucia still wound up dead. They'd had a good plan for getting the baby on a plane and Gil was still able to intercept her. The bottom line was any one of them might not make it back to the United States alive.

But in the same way that she'd mentally prepared herself for the trip to Colombia, Sonny ran through the steps needed for them to get to the boat. Gil had decided that Marco and Cooper would fly out of Cartagena and meet up with her parents, who were waiting for them in Miami.

"Sonny's already sent an e-mail to her dad telling him to expect a call from you once you two land in Miami," Gil added.

"That's right," Marco said to Sonny. "I'll fill your parents in on all the details once we land and we'll get right to work on chartering a boat."

Gil grabbed the suitcase and looked around the villa for anything that might give them away. There was nothing.

"We'll meet you somewhere in the Caribbean Sea in a few days," he said.

"Not me," Cooper said. "I get seasick. I'll be useless on a boat. I'll monitor things from Puerto Rico and liaison with the Coast Guard."

"Good."

"Then I'll get right on working out Cash Montgomery's whereabouts."

Sonny shot a look to Cooper and then to Gil. "You're not still searching for my brother, are you?"

He looked at her directly. She liked that about him.

He made no apologies for what he needed to do. He looked her square in the eye and gave her the truth.

"The job hasn't ended, Sonny. It's just taken a new turn."

She wouldn't let him see how it hurt her that he'd continue to pursue her brother after what had gone on between them last night. He'd held her, kissed her like he meant it. Yet his pursuit of her brother was something they couldn't resolve. Maybe ever.

"I won't waste my breath arguing with you about how wrong that is," she said.

Although she didn't know the details of Dylan's plan to rescue Cash, her parents did, and so did her future sister-in-law, Tammie. And as soon as Marco landed in Miami, he'd start grilling them about Cash. It was best she kept her mouth shut, taking things one step at a time.

"Good. Because we don't have time for it."

Sonny lifted her chin. "Then let's get going. The sooner we get out of Colombia, the better."

ELEVEN

They'd decided to leave the villa after Ellie had had her feeding and was sleepy. It was easier to transport her through town without drawing attention if she were asleep and not likely to laugh or cry. Gil had told them all that the enemy had many invisible faces. A smiling tourist who stopped to give attention to a laughing baby could easily contact a soldier to report seeing her.

When Ellie was awake she was curious, always looking around as if she didn't want to miss what was going on. But when she finally slept, she was out cold. What Sonny had mistaken for colic the first night was probably just Ellie's reaction to another change, another place, another stranger taking care of her.

Ellie seemed content now, tucked beneath Sonny's poncho. The fabric would shield Ellie from the hot afternoon sun. The muted colors allowed them to blend in with the scenery rather than make her stand out in a crowd.

Gil instructed them before they walked out the door to stay at ease. Sonny only wished she were feeling at ease about leaving the villa, no matter how much they needed to do it. They couldn't stay holed up there forever. But leaving the relative security these walls provided left them so exposed.

She climbed into the backseat of the car and Gil slipped in next to her. The car was hot from sitting in the sun. Even as they started to move, the breeze blowing in from the windows gave them little relief.

Sonny slipped the side of the poncho up, exposing the baby's face, but keeping her body and feet covered. If she woke up en route to the pier, it would make it easier to give her a bottle.

As they drove, Sonny's eyes darted from person to person on the streets, noting who turned to look at them as they passed.

"No one can see her in your lap," Gil said, sensing her anxiety. "As long as the car keeps moving, we'll be fine. Don't be nervous."

"How long is it going to take?"

"Not long. Olof is in a small pier in the old part of town. He moved his boat there this morning. There are too many boats moored at the marina where he was staying and more soldiers in that section of the city."

She nodded. "I just hope he's there."

Gil smiled, his eyes filled with warmth and reassurance. It didn't take away the nervous energy that was coursing through her, but knowing that he had her back made all the difference in the world.

They reached the old section of town near a park called Parque Simón Bolivar and immediately got stuck in traffic.

"Was there this much traffic on the street yesterday?" she asked, biting her bottom lip as she peered out the window at the crowd assembled in the park.

"I know you wanted to go the tourist route to blend in," Marco said, looking at them in the rearview mirror. "But we're going to get caught in all this traffic trying to make it to the coast."

"True. Take this right turn, Marco," Gil said, pointing to a small side road that looked like an alleyway. Only one car could pass down the road easily. "This should take us past San Pedro Claver Square and we'll only be a block or two from the pier."

Sonny drew in a deep breath and glanced down at Ellie. She was wiggling in her arms as if she were trying to get comfortable. Sweat made her downy hair stick to her forehead. Sonny lifted just a bit more so the light breeze from the window bathed her face.

Under different circumstances, Sonny would have loved to take in all the exquisite, old architectural features of the buildings in the old part of the city. She loved how each of the homes had second-story iron balconies, like the French Quarter in New Orleans. The buildings were painted in bright colors of red, butter-yellow and orange, reminding her of a sunset.

Many of the residents decorated their balconies with weathered urns filled with spectacularly colored flowers. The stucco walls of the buildings were cracked in places, with paint peeling and the color fading from the harsh rays of the Colombian sun. It was a sharp contrast to the modern buildings near the tourist area with beaches and hotels that reminded her of Miami.

She wouldn't be coming back to Colombia anytime soon, thank you very much. As beautiful as Cartagena was, the only memory she wanted to hold on to from this place was reaching into the basket in the back of

Torres's car and pulling Ellie into her arms for the first time.

No, that wasn't true, she decided, stealing a glance over at Gil. She had other memories to hold on to. She just wondered if she was still going to feel the same when they reached Miami. Gil's pursuit of her brother was relentless. If it were anyone else he was after, she'd admire his tenacity. But she wasn't going to allow anyone to interfere with Cash's rescue. Especially not in the name of money.

The car spilled out onto another busy road.

"This road is no better than the last," Marco said, glancing in the rearview mirror at Gil, his face steeped with worry. "Looks like they're having some kind of festival."

"No," Gil said, shifting forward in the seat to look out the front windshield. "They're checking cars."

"What?" Cooper said.

"Gil, I don't like this," Marco said.

"Don't worry. There are enough people on the streets for us to get lost in the crowd of tourists. The pier is just on the other side of the square on the inlet," Gil said.

In retrospect, it probably would've been better for them to wait until later in the evening to move. But they didn't have much of a choice. They'd been at the villa too long as it was.

"I still can't believe Eduardo Sanchez has the Colombian military in his back pocket the way he does," Marco said.

"He's one dangerous man. I want you to take us as close as you can to the pier. And try not to act so guilty, Marco," Gil said.

"Look at those machine guns. Is that an M16, Gil?" Marco asked.

"Keep your eyes on the road," Gil answered. "I'll keep an eye on the guns."

"Easy for you to say," Cooper said, gripping the seat. "You're going to need a lot of eyes out there, Gil. I've never seen this kind of manpower."

"I have," Gil said quietly. Sonny knew he was referring to his own duty in the Special Forces. He hadn't been very open about it. But Sonny understood that kind of silence well. Dylan had never wanted to share stories about his time in the military in any great detail.

"Are you okay, Cooper?" Sonny asked.

She drew in a deep breath. "Fine. Or I will be, when I get on that plane."

Gil closed his eyes for a brief moment. "You'll get there, Cooper."

"But what about you? I'm not sure I like this plan," Cooper said, glancing in the back. "Are you sure you can trust this Swedish guy?"

"No. But it's all we have to work with right now."

"Maybe Sonny can go alone with the baby? This Swedish guy should be able to take her out into the Gulf. I mean, he managed to cross the whole Atlantic in a boat all by himself. Sailing a few hundred miles across the Gulf shouldn't be a problem."

Gil shook his head. "What happens if something goes wrong? Sonny has the baby to think about. What is she going to do then?"

"She's in the car, you know," Sonny reminded them all. "Why do you people keep forgetting that one little fact?"

Gil smiled apologetically. "If something happens, I'll be right there. That's all I'm trying to say."

"Whoa," Cooper said, her hands braced against the dashboard. "Is that a roadblock?"

"If it isn't, it's disguised as a pretty good one," Marco said, searching down a side street a few hundred yards before the gridlock of cars ahead.

"Back up, Marco," Cooper said, turning to look over her shoulder at the traffic behind them.

"You have to go through it," Sonny said. "It'll look too suspicious if you try to turn here now."

"We'll get out here," Gil said, grabbing Sonny by the hand and opening the passenger door before the car came to a stop. "You won't have a problem going through the roadblock without us in the car."

"Wait, Gil, you can't get out here," Marco protested. "We're still a few blocks from the pier."

Cooper talked over him. "You're a sitting duck on the street. What if the baby wakes up?"

"We were sitting ducks as soon as I took Sonny and Ellie into the car with us at the airport. I'm not risking the two of you in that roadblock with Sonny and the baby in the car. Sonny's right. There's no place to turn the car around without it being obvious."

Marco banged his hand on the steering wheel. "I'm not leaving you out on the street, Gil."

"It's only a few more blocks. There's so much commotion going on outside, no one will notice us."

Cooper shook her head. "You don't know that for sure."

"No one does," Sonny said. "It's still safer than trying to get through that roadblock."

"Gil, the roadblock might not have anything to do with the baby at all. It could be some other random thing," Marco argued.

"I'm not taking that chance." Gil climbed out of the car, waited for Sonny and the baby to follow and then quickly slammed the door. "Get yourself out of Colombia and stick to the plan. If all goes well, we'll meet up in Puerto Rico at the end of the week."

The look on Marco's face stopped Sonny short. Did he really think he wasn't going to see his friend again? "Be careful," Marco said to them.

"Thank you both for everything," Sonny said to Marco and Cooper as she stood by the passenger side window. "You don't know how much I appreciate everything you've done—you're doing—for us."

"Good luck to both of you," Cooper said. "We'll see you in Puerto Rico in a week."

"Take care," Gil said. He took Sonny gently by the arm and moved her in the opposite direction, away from the roadblock.

Sonny reached beneath the poncho as she felt Ellie stir awake with her movement. Now that they were walking quickly through the crowded square toward the side street, the baby was being jostled around.

"She's waking up," she murmured to Gil.

"We're almost there."

They dodged the roadblock by going down an alleyway leading to the wall that surrounded the city.

Ellie started crying. Even though the sound was muffled beneath the poncho, her voice seemed to echo off the stone walls in the alley. When they emerged on the other side, Gil slowed her down.

There were military police everywhere, talking to the tourists.

"They can't be looking for us," Sonny said quietly, trying to shush Ellie at the same time. Her pulse thrummed loudly in her ear, drowning out the street noise.

"No. Something has happened here."

A man ran down the street past them, yelling in Spanish to a group of people. Although Sonny knew Spanish well, the dialect and the urgency with which the man spoke made it difficult for her to understand every word.

"Someone has been killed," she said, her body limp with dread. "There's a body."

"It doesn't concern us. Keep moving. We still have to get through this street before we reach—"

Gil stopped short.

"What is it?"

"There weren't any guards down at the pier earlier. Let's go this way. We may be able to go around them."

They walked through crowded San Pedro Claver Square. The baby was now awake and fussing loudly. Although Sonny knew the poncho would protect her from the harsh heat of the sun, it was still hot under there.

Gil looked at her, and at the wiggling poncho.

"She's awake," Sonny said, trying desperately to keep her voice from revealing the alarm she felt.

A woman at the market turned at the sound of Ellie crying.

"Keep her quiet," Gil said, his voice low. "Give her a bottle if you have to."

"How can I do that without drawing attention?"

"Quickly." He took her by the hand and moved faster. Sonny had to practically run to keep up with him. She held her hand steady on Ellie's back.

Soldiers were at every stairway leading down to the pier where they were to meet Olof. One soldier clearly heard Ellie's cries and raised his gun.

Without thought, Sonny pulled Gil in the direction of a large church. Gil seemed to know what she was thinking and didn't resist. With one hand gripping his suitcase and the other on the small of her back, he moved her quickly over the brick and concrete streets, weaving in between people in the square, ignoring the shouts of the soldiers at their backs.

Gil pushed through the door of the church and led her into the quiet, leaving the commotion behind them outside. It took a moment for her eyes to adjust to the change of light. The inside of the church was cool. With a quick movement, she lifted the poncho off Ellie and unleashed the baby's cries. The sound of her distress echoed off the walls of the church.

As the noise outside drew closer, a priest appeared at the altar, curious about what was happening just outside the door.

Taking Sonny by the hand, Gil pulled her toward the altar. "Sanctuary! Please give us sanctuary!"

TWELVE

They hurried to the front of the church. It broke Sonny's heart that Ellie was upset, but she couldn't stop to soothe her.

"Why do you need sanctuary?" the priest asked, his accent evident even though he spoke perfect English.

"We need to get to the pier," Gil said as he reached into his bag for the bottle they'd prepared before they left. "There are too many soldiers roaming the streets."

The priest nodded his head. "Yes, I know. They're questioning people in the murder of a man found in an alleyway. He was a prominent businessman."

"I see," Sonny said, closing her eyes as the news sunk in. They weren't after her and Ellie. Marco had been right. It had nothing to do with them. At least for now. Gil handed her the bottle and she quickly gave it to Ellie to silence her.

"That's too bad," Gil said. "May we stay here a while to get cool?"

The priest smiled, yet questions remained in his expression. "Stay as long as you like. If there's anything—" His attention was pulled toward the church doors as a soldier stepped inside.

"Excuse me, please," the priest said, and then went to talk to the soldier.

"Keep your face toward the front," Gil said.

Sonny sat down on the old bench and pulled the poncho off her body slowly. Gil followed and sat down next to her, sliding the suitcase in front of the bench to hide it.

"We'll be safe here for a while," Gil whispered as she held Ellie in her arms.

Reaching over, he brushed his hand over Ellie's forehead to wipe off the sweat and smooth back her hair. Ellie was drinking as if she hadn't had a bottle in days. Every so often she'd choke and cough from taking in too much too fast.

"She was really thirsty," Sonny whispered, closing her eyes, trying not to think about the soldier in the church.

"Are you listening to what they're saying?"

"What?"

"The priest is saying the soldiers are not to come into the church except to pray," he whispered.

Sonny hadn't been paying attention. But now that the baby was quiet, she could make out their words.

"Just because the guards won't touch us while we're in the church doesn't mean we're safe. We can't stay here forever, Gil. At some point we need to leave. Who knows if Olof will wait for us?"

"He will. He needs the money. And I don't intend for us to stay here any longer than we need to. The soldiers may honor the sanctity of these church walls, but they're going to get antsy and make a move eventually. I don't want to give them enough time to make a plan." Gil stole a glance backward to see the soldier leave. The priest stayed by the door, watching the activity outside. "The soldier's gone."

He turned back to her and their eyes met in a way that spoke of understanding. "This is going to get a lot worse before it gets better, isn't it?" she asked.

Gil's jaw clenched. "Not if I can help it."

She touched his arm, letting her hand linger there, but said nothing more. She wanted to tell him that he was just one man. That he could only do so much. The rest they had to let go of and put in God's hands.

Instead, she nodded.

Ellie had pulled away from the bottle and was babbling happily. The sound of her glee rang out in the church.

Left alone with his thoughts, Gil's face looked serene, unmarred by the worry she'd seen all day.

"What are you thinking of?" she whispered, wondering if she should disturb him.

He looked at her and sighed. "Just praying."

Her eyes widened.

He smirked. "Don't act so surprised."

"I'm not. It's just…" Suddenly stunned by her initial assessment that Gil was not a praying man, Sonny felt herself shrink. She should know better than to prejudge a person. His initial reaction to her putting her faith in God had her thinking that he was a nonbeliever. Clearly she'd been mistaken.

"I've never been comfortable being open with my faith. But I'm almost ashamed to say that it's something I've let slip away from me for a while now."

"You don't have to explain."

He smiled. "I know I don't. And I don't want you to

think I just come to the Lord when I'm in crisis. It was actually a crisis in my life that had me questioning some things."

"Bruce?"

He chuckled. "You and Cooper must have had quite a conversation about me."

"She wasn't gossiping."

"I know. That's not her way."

"She said you still feel responsible."

He gave a slight shrug of his shoulder. "Yeah, well, that's a thing I do. But it wasn't Bruce. I'd backed away long before he was killed."

"What was it?"

"It doesn't really matter why. Only that I did."

Her expression was filled with empathy. He cleared his throat.

"I went to one of the other churches yesterday," he said, looking around. "The cathedral. Cartagena has some beautiful churches."

"Really?"

"Yeah. I was walking and trying to figure out what I could have done differently to protect my team. To protect you and Ellie. I just walked inside and sat there like this. It felt good just sitting. I wasn't praying, I was just sitting there and no one paid me any mind. It had been a long time since I'd been inside the walls of a church."

She let Gil talk, keeping her own thoughts to herself. Sometimes the only way to let God in was to just get out of His way.

"He's innocent, isn't he?" Gil said quietly. "Your brother?"

Sonny closed her eyes as a rush of emotion enveloped her. To have someone on her side for a change was overwhelming. "Yes."

"Can he prove it?"

"No. Not yet, anyway."

She saw his shoulders slump. "Then you all have quite the fight ahead of you."

"I believe he knew that. Cash has never backed down from a fight."

"Hè's a brave man to be an army of one against the DEA."

She glanced down at the baby, who was looking up at the ornate ceiling. "He's not fighting against the DEA. There's someone behind it all. Just one man or maybe a few. I don't know. Manuel Turgis and Eduardo Sanchez are only part of it. It wouldn't be so hard to fight if we could just see their faces and know what they're truly after."

"That's a mighty tall order."

"Then we'll reach high."

He chuckled. In the quiet of the church, it seemed to boom. "I wish I had your kind of faith."

She smiled as she looked at him. "You might surprise yourself."

He paused, and his face changed. "You know I'm going to have to take Cash in when I find him, Sonny."

"You don't mean you're still going to go after him."

"Not right now, no. But when I get you and Ellie to safety, I'm going back out."

She sighed. "Why do you need to do this? You just admitted you believe in his innocence. You know he's not guilty of these crimes he's been accused of."

"My belief isn't enough. The only way he can prove his innocence is if he comes in to face justice."

She looked at him hard. "His bondsman must really be paying a lot for his return."

"It's not about the money."

"Isn't it?"

Gil sighed. "At first it was. It's what I do, Sonny. It's how I make my living. When you have money like that dangled in front of you, it's hard to pass it up. That's my burden to bear in all this. I wanted that bounty and look where it got me—and you."

He draped his arm across the back of the seat and touched her hair. "I can't help but think how my greed put you in harm's way."

She spoke soberly. "It's out of our hands. If we could go back and change things, we could keep my brother from ever getting arrested. Go back even further and we could keep Ellie's grandfather from working with Aztec Corporation and putting the family in danger in the first place.

"Don't you see? You'd have to keep going back to change things. You can't do that. You can only move forward. You can't change what Manuel Turgis and Eduardo Sanchez have done to my family."

"Did I hear you say Manuel Turgis?"

Sonny turned to find the priest standing at the end of the aisle. She'd been lost in the conversation she'd been having with Gil, encompassed by the safety of the church walls.

"Did you know him?" the priest asked them with interest.

Gil turned in his seat, his body acting like a shield. "Why?"

"The soldiers are searching for anyone with a con-nection to the man whose body they found in the alley."

"Let me guess," Gil said. "His name was Manuel Turgis."

The streets of Cartagena were dark when they finally emerged from the back door of the church. The priest led them to a stone path that brought them to the pier. It was well past midnight and the activity that had domi-nated the street had vanished.

"You'll need to be careful," the priest said. "There may be some soldiers on this path, in the shadows. It is sometimes guarded to prevent crime."

"I appreciate all your help," Sonny said. "And thank you for not giving us away to the soldiers."

The pastor looked at Ellie, then at Sonny. "Colombia has its law to follow. But I follow the Lord's law. Stay safe on your journey."

"Thank you," Gil said.

Sonny didn't feel as sure-footed as she wanted to, taking the footpath down to the small pier at the end of a private beach.

"Do you think anyone saw us?" she asked Gil.

"Let's hope not. It wouldn't be anyone we'd want to meet."

They reached a stairway that led to a tunnel. From the small light Gil held in his hand, she could see the red tile on the floor and green moss growing up the cement walls. It was damp and hot, and no place she'd ever think of venturing on her own.

"Take my hand. There's no railing," he said, holding a hand out to help her down the stairs.

The chill of the cement underground seeped into her bones, mingling with the chill of fear. She walked quickly to keep up with Gil. The baby babbled beneath her poncho, warm against Sonny's body, protected from the chill and wondering eyes.

"The pier is just beyond these stairs."

As they emerged from the tunnel, he pulled her close, draping his arm around her and slowing his pace.

"Stay close to me," he said, walking with her like a couple in love would do. "I hear voices."

"They'll hear the baby," she said quietly, looking up into his eyes. The moon that had been so bright last night was hidden behind clouds. But she could see his eyes shining back at her. She loved their dark-brown color and the way they looked at her intently. Now they were stormy and showed the gravity of their situation.

"No one will notice us, unless we give them a reason. We're almost there."

As they reached the beach, the small pier came into view. Although there were two boats moored against the dock, only one boat was lit up. The ghostly looking sailboat that was tied to the other side looked abandoned.

"Good, he's here," Gil said. "I wasn't sure he'd wait with all the commotion in the square this afternoon. Don't worry. We'll be safe."

Sonny nodded. But nothing was really going to feel safe to her except standing on solid ground in Puerto Rico. She couldn't help but wonder what she'd find when they reached the boat.

Keep me, O Lord, from the hands of the wicked; preserve me from the violent man who has purposed to overthrow my goings.

"Are you ready for this?" Gil asked, breaking into her quiet reflection.

"Do we have a choice?" He said nothing, which was answer enough. "There's no way out of Colombia for us, except by boat, right?"

"Yes," he said honestly.

"Are there still pirates in these waters?"

"Possibly. There hasn't been an attack on Cartagena in a long time but out there on the water… Boats have been known to be overtaken by pirates."

He held her gently by the upper arm and looked into her eyes.

"Sonny, there's no other way. I know you're scared, but remember, Olof doesn't have loyalty to Eduardo Sanchez or anyone else who might be looking for us. We're just tourists to him and he's just a sailor who wants to make some money."

She sighed. After all this, how could she be such a coward? "Once we're on that boat, there's nowhere to run."

"You're right. But you're going to be with me. And I'm not going to leave you. You can be sure of that. Come on."

His words gave her some measure of comfort and, despite her fear, she felt a smile tug at her lips. When her feet hit the rough weathered boards of the dock, she said, "If I have to be doing this with someone, I'm glad it's you."

Gil stopped and turned to her. "Are you sure?"

"Positive. Since I've been in Colombia, I've prayed to the Lord for safekeeping. I think He answered me by sending you."

"Lest you forget, I'm the one that kept you from getting on the plane to Miami."

"I'm not talking about the plane."

She gazed up into his eyes and saw him grasp what she was trying to tell him. She felt a connection to him so powerful that it rivaled the force of a hurricane.

"Hey, we have Him on our side, too," she said. "Between you and the Lord, how much more safe can a girl be?"

She felt his smile against her lips as he kissed her. It wasn't that quick, sharp kiss she'd given him at the airport when they'd been detained by the guards. This one was gentle, steeped with emotion that threatened to sweep her away and make her forget her reason. Just like the kiss they'd shared in the courtyard last night.

She knew she was safe following this man wherever he led.

THIRTEEN

Sonny's lips were as soft as he remembered. The warm air of the Caribbean Sea stirred her hair around her face as he kissed her. This felt good and right and where he wanted to be. Yet there was still so much uncertainty ahead of them—he had to stay focused. So he reluctantly pulled away.

Finding his voice, he looked into her eyes. "We need to go. I want to be out at sea before first light. Far enough away so that we aren't visible from the shore."

Sonny's eyes glowed from the moonlight. Her lips were moist from their kiss and he resisted the urge to touch them. He wanted to hold her in his arms. He loved the way she fit so perfectly against him. But this wasn't the right time.

"Okay," she said, her voice as gentle as the warm breeze bathing him. "Let's do it."

"You amaze me."

"I do?"

"Your conviction that everything is going to be all right is so strong," he said. "You don't waver at all. You're ready for anything."

"Not anything. There are a lot of things I'm not ready to face. And I won't. That makes me a coward."

He chuckled. "I don't think anyone would use the word *coward* to describe you, Sonny Montgomery."

He took her by the arm and led her down the quiet dock, unsure of what lay ahead of them.

Gil knew the Lord would be a guide for them and that her feelings of faith were strong. He just wasn't sure he was worthy of her faith in *him*. Especially since he had no idea if they'd ever make it to Puerto Rico.

"You never mentioned anything about a kid and a woman when we talked," Olof said to Gil as a way of introduction.

He was a man tall in height and short in small talk, Sonny decided as the wiry man stood on deck.

Olof stared at Sonny. His gaze didn't make her skin crawl but it filled her with enough uneasiness to put her on edge. Was this really a good idea?

"Didn't I?" Gil said. "I thought I had. Why? Is that going to be a problem?"

Olof hesitated, then said, "No, no problem. Except I don't have provisions for the little one. There's enough food here to last adults a month, though."

"I brought baby food with me," Sonny said.

"Hmm, well, that's good. We're going to have to think of a way to store those dirty diapers. Gets crowded in the cabin real fast and clean air is precious. But I think I have enough plastic bags to handle it for a few days."

She bit her lip, her eyes shifting from Olof's skeptical face to the thirty-foot sailboat they were about to board. The *Kia II* looked as if it had weathered many storms.

"Don't worry yourself about my girl. She may not seem like much of a boat, but she's seaworthy. Strong and steady," Olof said in his Swedish accent, reading Sonny's mind.

"It's a beautiful boat," she said. It wouldn't do her any good to offend her captain before they even set sail.

"*Kia II* is named after my late wife. Her name means 'follower of Christ.'"

Sonny smiled, relaxing a bit. "That's lovely."

"She was," he said warmly.

"Do you maintain her yourself?" Gil asked.

"When I can. I know her inside and out. Don't you worry. She'll get you where you're going. Well, don't just stand there. Hop on board. We'll take care of business and then I'll show you around before we shove off."

If this was what she had to do, Sonny was up for it. She'd seen it this far, she'd see it the rest of the way. No matter how rickety the boat felt beneath her feet when she climbed on deck.

"So, you're headed to Puerto Rico, huh? Ever been there?"

"Yes," Gil answered, extending his hand to shake Olof's in greeting. "When I was in the military. I was stationed there for about six months."

"So have I," Olof said, gripping Gil's hand in turn. "It's a pretty island. So long as I'm not bringing fugitives into the country, we're fine. I like my freedom to come and go. Don't want the U.S. to suddenly ban me from their borders. You know what I mean?"

"We have a boat from the U.S. meeting us halfway," Sonny said. "We know you don't want to take us the whole way in."

Olof motioned to the bag Gil was holding. It was filled with baby essentials for the next few days.

"I don't mean to be suspicious or anything, but there were a lot of soldiers crawling that wall through the afternoon. Do you mind if I take a look in your bag? You know, just to make sure?"

Gil unzipped the overnight suitcase. "Go right ahead. We don't have anything to hide."

Olof scrutinized the bag, moving various sundries around to view the full contents. Satisfied, he zipped the bag shut.

He shrugged as if embarrassed. "You can never be too careful. I don't want any drugs on my boat. Don't need that kind of trouble."

"I understand completely and I agree." Gil reached into a zippered pocket on the bag and pulled out an envelope. "Here's half the money. When the other boat meets us midway in the Caribbean Sea at the coordinates we've agreed on, you'll get the rest."

With a quick check of the bills in the envelope, Olof nodded. "Much appreciated. It'll go a long way toward my journey back home."

"I'm just glad you were available to help us," Sonny said.

"As long as the boat meets us at the right coordinates, we should have an uneventful trip. You can sit back and let yourself enjoy the beautiful Caribbean Sea. I hope you brought your sunscreen," he said, turning to Sonny. "The sun's reflection off the water will give you sunburn like you've never had before. Make sure you keep the baby covered up. Don't want the little one to get a burn."

He pocketed the envelope and turned toward the stairway leading down to the cabin. "Let's get you settled. I cleaned out the front bunk, figuring you could use it since you're the paying guest. Oftentimes I sleep in the bow. The seat cushions there convert into a bed."

When he got to the bottom of the stairs he turned and squinted his eyes as Gil descended the stairs. "I barely make it in there myself and I'm about your size. I'm not sure if the lot of you are going to fit."

"Give the bunk to my wife and the baby," Gil said, looking at Sonny.

Olof shrugged. "There's plenty of room in the main cabin to make another bed. The *Kia II* sleeps five people fairly comfortably." Glancing at the baby he added with a chuckle, "It can handle three and a half when they're this small."

He smiled and the unrest that Sonny had felt before boarding seemed to wash away.

"Don't know why you didn't decide to just take a plane back to the U.S. Cartagena has a nice airport. Miami is only a two-and-a-half-hour flight. Much quicker than sailing."

"I haven't quite conquered my fear of flying," Sonny said, holding back a grimace at her fib. "I just barely made it through the flight down."

That much was true, she thought, recalling how nerve-racking her flight to Colombia had been in anticipation of what she was about to do.

"Just barely," Gil chimed in, as if to give credence to her story and appease the curiosity of their captain. "I still have the fingernail marks in my arm to prove it."

Olof laughed loud. "Women."

Sonny bristled inside. She hated blanket comments aimed to put down women. If he only knew the truth, he'd think differently. But he never would know because she wasn't about to tell him.

"You'll be comfortable in that front bunk. Holler if you need anything."

"Is it safe to sail at night?" Sonny asked.

Olof looked at Gil and then Sonny. "You're not nervous about sailing, are you?"

"No."

Olof moved aside to let Sonny pass. "Good. To make the kind of time you want to make and meet the other boat on time, we'll need to do some night sailing. Don't you worry, though. I've been sailing since before you were born."

Sonny took in the bunk at the front of the ship. She had no idea if it was starboard, port or bow since she didn't know what those terms meant. But it didn't really matter. The bunk was private and gave her plenty of room to sleep with Ellie right beside her.

Gil poked his head inside. "Why don't you try to get some rest. It's been a long day." He dropped the bag on the mattress. "Are you okay?" he asked quietly.

"I'm just eager to get out to sea. I want to get home."

He reached up and traced his fingers along her jaw, caressing her cheek with his thumb. Her head grew light and she leaned into his touch.

"We'll be home soon. You can sleep easy tonight."

Gil rolled out the blankets Olof had left for him on the cushions. He felt better sleeping on the other side of the wall from Sonny and Ellie. Call it his overprotective nature, but he wanted to be right there in case Sonny called for him.

Although they'd chosen to sail during the night, they couldn't sail at a fast clip. They had to be careful. In the Caribbean, most charter companies forbid sailing at night, but since Olof owned his own vessel and was an experienced sailor, they kept the jib up.

Gil punched the pillow and looked out the porthole toward the shoreline. Lights were still visible in the city. In a matter of time they'd fade in the distance. By the time they woke up tomorrow morning, Cartagena would be a distant memory.

It would be a two-and-a-half-day sail to the coordinates he'd given Olof. With any luck, they'd be meeting either Marco or Sonny's father with another boat that would bring them the rest of the way to Ponce, Puerto Rico. The total trip would take four to five days if they didn't hit a snag.

And if they did, they could always call the U.S. Coast Guard in Puerto Rico to help. He only hoped there wouldn't be a need for that.

He stretched out on the bed and pulled the light blanket over him. Four or five days was all he had left with Sonny before the reality of their lives crashed down around them. It seemed too short a time and yet the amount of time they'd already spent together was half that. Given how much he felt for her, it didn't seem possible.

He glanced at the closed door to the bunk. Sonny and Ellie were sleeping soundly inside. At least he hoped Sonny was sleeping. It would be good if at least one of them had a good night's sleep. Gil had the feeling he wouldn't truly rest at all until they set foot on the sands of Ponce.

Sonny bent down and blew a raspberry on Ellie's stomach. The baby responded by giggling loudly and kicking her legs wildly as if she was doing top-speed aerobics.

"I think you've grown an inch in the last few days! I must be feeding you well."

The smile on Sonny's face wilted just a little. If Sonny could see the change after just a few days, she knew Serena would see an enormous change in her daughter. And Cash wouldn't even recognize Ellie.

What had Ellie been—barely a month old—when she was taken? Now at almost five months old, she'd changed so drastically from the picture Serena had given her that Ellie looked like a different baby.

Sonny watched her wiggling and squealing, almost begging Sonny to kiss her belly again. No, Cash would recognize Ellie. How could he not? She looked just like their mother.

She heard Olof and Gil on the deck of the boat. At first, it just sounded like they were talking. But Sonny realized that Gil's voice was raised in what sounded like anger.

Sonny grabbed Ellie, leaning her against the blanket on her shoulder, and climbed the stairs carefully, holding one hand on the baby and one on the railing.

"What's going on?" she asked when she made it on deck.

"We've got company," Gil said, eyeing Olof.

Sonny's heart leaped. "My father?"

"No," Gil said, staring out at the small pebble-sized boat in the distance. He grabbed the binoculars and looked in the direction of the small boat.

Sonny pulled the small blanket over Ellie's head to protect her from the sun. "How do you know?"

"I can't get them to answer on the radio," Gil said.

"It still could be my father," she said, feeling hopeful. "Maybe he's just being cautious." She knew her father would move mountains to get to her if he could.

It had been four days since they'd left Cartagena. They should have met her father yesterday afternoon—that is, if Marco had been able to get in touch with him. The wind hadn't been on their side during the trip, slowing down their progress. Even so, they should have connected with her father by now.

"And maybe it's someone who doesn't want us to know they're coming," Gil said.

"You're overreacting. It's probably just a charter boat with a novice captain," Olof insisted. "It's nothing."

Gil dropped the binoculars down on the shelf. "That's no charter cruise."

Worried, Sonny asked, "How do you know?"

"Because I've never known sunbathers out for a good time to pack weapons with their sunscreen. Let's get the sails up."

"I'd feel better if you both went below," Olof said.

"Sonny, take the baby below and get her ready in the carrier in case we need to board another boat quickly. Go on," Gil said. "I'll stay on deck."

Her heart hammered and she clutched the baby tighter. The trip this far had been uneventful. She'd spent yesterday sunning on deck while Ellie slept in the bunk below. She'd felt so good by last night that she'd made dinner for all of them. Not once had there been any sign of Sanchez's men following them, but that didn't mean they wouldn't.

Dear Lord, please let this be my father in that boat. Please don't let it be someone here to take Ellie.

She said her prayer over and over as she set the baby down in the makeshift crib she'd built to keep Ellie from rolling around the bunk. They hadn't brought too much with them, and even if they did, Sonny didn't have time to gather it. Instead, she quickly dressed Ellie, then strapped the baby carrier on before slipping the baby inside.

"Sonny!" Gil called, as the pitch of the boat suddenly shifted. It began to rock in a way it hadn't since they'd been on board, making it more difficult for her to move. She was glad Ellie was in her front carrier—she wouldn't have been able to hold on to her and keep her hands supported on the cabinet above as the boat rocked.

She made her way through the galley kitchen. "I'm coming."

"No, stay down there."

Puzzled, she peered up the stairs leading to the deck. Olof had a gun, but instead of pointing at the fast moving boat, he aimed it at Gil. She gasped, and her hand protectively went to the baby.

"I changed my mind. I'm going to need you up here, little lady."

Gil didn't look at her. Instead, his eyes were fixed on the gun directed at him.

"Why are you doing this?" she asked, as she climbed the stairs.

"Get behind me with the baby," Gil said, holding out his hand and guiding her to a place where he could shield them.

Olof shrugged. "I'm sorry. I am, really. But I'm a businessman, too."

"I don't understand," Sonny said, looking around. The main sail had been dropped and the fabric was flapping in the wind because it hadn't been tied down. The jib had been rolled in. "What's going on here? Why did we stop?"

Gil's voice was cold. "My guess is Eduardo Sanchez has already gotten to him."

"The word in Cartagena is that you're fugitives and that you stole that baby. I'm merely making sure the baby is returned to her rightful parents."

Sonny closed her eyes at the irony of it.

"I'm sure the money they're offering doesn't hurt, either," Gil said.

"I'd be lying if I said that wasn't a factor. It's significantly more than you offered to pay me. It costs a lot of money to do what I do, sailing around the world."

"We could get you more," Sonny pleaded. She knew Serena had more money in her trust fund. She'd willingly hand over the entire Davco fortune to get Ellie back.

"I'm sure Eduardo or one of his people made you some offer you couldn't refuse," Gil asked quietly. "Who was it? Manuel Turgis?"

"I saw the news. Sanchez is loaded," Olof replied, shrugging. "When Turgis came to me to find out if anyone had chartered a boat, I figured I could just bypass him and go straight to the source."

"Did you kill Manuel Turgis?" Sonny asked.

"He wouldn't pay me what I wanted."

Sonny's mouth dropped open. "Just like that. He didn't give you what you wanted so you killed him and contacted Eduardo Sanchez?"

Olof nodded. "Sanchez was a bit more agreeable than Mr. Turgis. Like I said, I'm a businessman. Why not make it as profitable as I could by going straight to the top instead of working with the middleman?"

"How could you trade a little baby for money!" Sonny cried.

"You can't blame me."

"I can, actually," said Sonny.

Gil kept his hand out to shield Sonny and the baby as best he could. "I never mentioned anything about Sonny and Ellie coming with me on this trip, but this deal was made before we left Cartagena. How did you know?"

"I put it together. I asked myself why you'd be willing to pay so much money to leave Cartagena with me when you could easily have chartered a much nicer boat for much less. Or boarded a plane that could take you anywhere. You had something to hide. Or rather, *someone* to hide. But even if I hadn't figured it out, it wouldn't have changed anything."

"Why not?" Sonny asked.

"They came to me. They already knew you'd hired me. But they weren't sure you'd have the baby with you."

The boat rocked and Sonny lost her balance. Gil grabbed her arm from behind as she slid onto a deck cushion. Her position gave her a better view of the oncoming boat. Her heart raced as it approached.

"There was talk on the street that Eduardo Sanchez was looking for a baby. I didn't know this baby was the one he was looking for until I radioed in some information. As luck would have it—"

"Luck?" Sonny said. "Do you have any idea the kind of man you're dealing with?"

"No," Gil said, looking directly at Olof. "If he did, he never would have taken the job."

Olof shrugged. "Nothing personal. They would have killed me for not cooperating. This way, I get paid."

Gil laughed humorlessly. "You don't really expect them to let any of us live after they take the baby, do you, Olof? Especially after what you did to Turgis?"

The boat was getting closer. Sonny fought to keep her breathing even.

"You sat at dinner with us last night. You laughed with us. You told us about your wife's cancer. And all the while you were planning to give us up?" The betrayal Sonny felt over Olof's turn of loyalty was harsh.

Sonny heard the engine of the boat, but could no longer see it behind Olof.

"Gil?" she said quietly, fearing Eduardo's men would board the boat at any moment. But neither Gil nor Olof seemed to be paying attention.

"You shouldn't have gotten in over your head," Olof argued.

"You think you haven't?" Gil asked.

"That's not for you to worry about. You have other worries ahead of you when I hand you all over to—"

He stopped short as he realized the other boat was coming into view. In the split second Olof turned to look at the other boat, Gil moved into action. The first hit dropped the gun to the floor. The next one sent Olof facedown on deck.

Sonny turned and saw the catamaran breezing toward them at a good clip from the other direction. Excitement bubbled up inside her, but was replaced with terror as gunshots rang out over her head.

"Get ready to board!" her father called out. "I'm going to swing around!"

"Dad!"

Gil pulled Sonny to her feet. "Hold on. I'm going to get the raft ready and when he swings around we'll catch him. Get a life jacket on."

"Gil, we're not going to make it. The other boat will get here first," she said, pulling the cushion off the bench to access the storage unit where the life jackets were housed.

"Just get ready to board the raft. It's going to be tight but we'll make it."

He picked up the gun he'd knocked from Olof's hand, checked for bullets and then slipped the gun into his waistband.

"You'll never outrun their boat in a life raft," Olof said, holding his head and rolling on the deck.

"We won't be outrunning them in the raft."

With a yank of the cord, the raft inflated easily enough.

Gil climbed down to the raft first and tied it to the side of the ladder to make it easier for Sonny to climb down.

In the few seconds it took for Sonny to pull the life jacket over her, she realized it would be of no use to her. Not while Ellie was still in the carrier. If she fell into the water, her head would remain above water. But Ellie's wouldn't.

"I have them," Olof yelled.

Drawn to the ruckus on the other side of the boat, Sonny turned her head. "Gil! They've boarded!"

Bullets exploded near her and she instinctively threw her arms around Ellie to protect her.

"She has the baby! Don't shoot." Sonny heard someone yell in a commanding voice from the other boat.

"Come on, Sonny! Jump!"

Startled by Gil's command, Sonny turned and descended the stairs, fearing she'd somehow drop the baby. Her heart hammered wildly in her chest but Gil's strong hands reached up and guided her onto the raft. She fell into the raft on her back with the baby secure in her carrier on top of her.

They had no protection from the powerboat that had just slid alongside Olof's sailboat. Since it was still in motion, it glided past Olof's boat for a good distance and swung around.

Two of Eduardo's men were on board Olof's boat with guns at the ready. But it was the man standing on the powerboat, glaring at the raft with contempt, that stopped Sonny's breathing. She couldn't believe her eyes.

"Eduardo Sanchez is on that boat. He won't risk them shooting at the raft," Gil said.

Gil took the oars and rowed out, away from both

Olof's and Sanchez's boats, giving the Catamaran her father had chartered a wide berth for when he swung around again. Sonny trusted her father and she'd put all her trust in Gil. Still, she closed her eyes as the catamaran sped toward them.

Sonny could hear the men yelling from Sanchez's boat, and gunshots rang out again. She shielded Ellie as best she could, though she couldn't tell if they were shooting at the raft to deflate it, or shooting at her father. Both options were terrifying.

Sonny opened her eyes to find the catamaran speeding toward them even faster, but they were still too far away to board. The sails were down and only the motor was moving the boat. Even when her father cut the engine, the boat continued to glide toward them disturbingly fast.

"Throw me the line!" Gil called out. Turning to Sonny, he instructed, "Keep yourself down and shield the baby. I don't want you to get hit with the buoy. We only have one shot at this."

The gunned engine of the powerboat grew louder. Sonny could see that Eduardo was headed for Olof's boat to pick up the men who had boarded.

Rolling to her side, she covered Ellie with her body and felt the rope connect with the side of the raft just as a wave from the wake of the catamaran lifted the raft. Ellie giggled, unaffected by the commotion around her.

When she finally dared to look up, she saw Gil holding the lifeline that connected their small raft to the catamaran. When the rope became taut, the raft lifted on one end and started to move.

"Hold on. We're almost there."

Within minutes, between her father and Gil's efforts,

the raft reached the catamaran. And then the gunshots started again.

"Hand her to me!" her father said. Sonny had never been so happy to see him in all her life. Tears stung her eyes, making it hard to see.

"I have her, Dad," she sobbed.

Gil steadied the raft as best he could while Sonny climbed the steps on the back of the catamaran to deck. Her father grabbed her by the hands and then pulled her into his arms.

"I'm so happy to see you," she cried.

"There's no time for reunions now, sweetie. Take the baby downstairs to the aft bunk. We've still got company," he said as a bullet lodged in the raft and the air escaped with a violent hiss.

FOURTEEN

Gil pulled himself on board the catamaran as the raft began to sink. If he'd been quicker and a little steadier on his feet, he would have missed the left hook that connected with his jaw.

"Daddy!" he heard Sonny scream as he stumbled backward. "What are you doing?"

"That's for putting my little girl in danger. Now help me get us out of here."

Gil rubbed his jaw with his hand, opening his mouth to test the damage. He'd survive but he'd be feeling that punch for a while and he wasn't so sure he didn't deserve it.

"Sonny, listen to your father and take the baby down below. And pray. I think we're going to need it," Gil said.

"But you may need my help."

"We can't worry about you and Ellie on deck while we try to outrun this boat," her father said. "Just keep Ellie next to you but out of the way of anything that might get knocked over. This ride might get a little rough."

"Okay," she said.

When she turned to head for the cabin, she paused,

leaned toward Gil and kissed him. If she saw the daggers her father's eyes threw at him, she ignored them and took Ellie down to the main cabin.

"Where are they, sir?" he said, looking the man straight in the eyes. Not with challenge but with determination to see this through.

"Coming in fast. We need to get this boat turned back around." He gestured to the gun Gil had taken from Olof. "Do you know how to use that gun you've got tucked in your pants?"

"Four years in Army Special Forces, sir. Seven years in law enforcement."

A look of admiration crossed his face. "Good. There are two rifles hanging by the radio in the cockpit. Use them if you have to. Anything comes close to this boat, shoot it!"

"You got it."

Gil followed behind him, matching his step as he lifted the main sail. If the past few days on Olof's boat had taught him anything, it was his way around the deck of a sailboat. With all the sails raised and the catamaran turned into the wind, they took off.

As they started to move, Gil turned back to gauge the distance between them and the boat pursuing them.

"This boat may not look like much, but the gentleman I chartered her from said she could fly."

That's good, Gil thought. They needed to fly if they had any chance of reaching Puerto Rico alive.

Sonny walked through the catamaran's cabin until she found a bunk. The boat was moving quickly and she had to hold on to the wall until she was able to sit down on the edge of the bed. She used the outer wall as leverage so she could take Ellie out of the carrier.

"Come here, Ellie," she said after freeing her. "Come snuggle with me and say a prayer."

She heard her father's voice mingling with Gil's as they shouted information to one another.

Anything comes close to this boat, shoot it. That's what her father had said. The thought of more shooting terrified her. The image of Lucia's body slumped over and the metallic smell of blood flooded her memory. *Lord, please take care of my father and Gil.*

A tear trickled down her cheek. Ellie was looking around at her new surroundings. Oh, what a blessed comfort this little baby was to her. Ellie was completely unaware of what it had taken to get her back. She was just a baby and with the Lord's help, she would have no memories of this nightmare to carry through her life.

But Sonny would never forget a moment of the past few weeks. *Especially these past few days with Gil.*

A shot rang out on deck and she heard a high-pitched ping, signaling the bullet had hit something on the boat. More shots, louder than the first, sounded above her.

Eduardo Sanchez had looked straight into her eyes with a kind of contempt she'd never seen. He was responsible for so much pain. He'd threatened Serena's family her whole life, he'd been responsible for Cash's disappearance and he'd taken Ellie from them all.

A chill raced up her spine with the memory of his eyes staring at her. She had the baby now. He couldn't hurt Ellie anymore. She closed her eyes and prayed for Cash and for her father and Gil, who were still in the line of fire.

It killed her not to know what was happening on deck. But she couldn't put Ellie in danger by leaving her here to check. What if something happened? Who would take care of the baby?

And what about Gil? The very thought of losing him nearly broke her in two.

Fear for her father and for the man she was falling in love with overwhelmed her. Hadn't they all lost enough? Didn't she and Gil deserve a chance to see where these feelings would take them?

Gil had told her to get down in the cabin and pray. She curled herself up in a ball and hugged Ellie to her chest. And she prayed. She prayed for her father, her brothers and for Gil. She hoped that God would give them all another chance at happiness.

Gil had radioed the Coast Guard their coordinates, telling them the catamaran was under attack by pirates. But waiting for reinforcements to arrive while trying to outrun Sanchez's men was maddening. Sonny's father steered the thirty-five foot catamaran, catching as much wind as he could with the sails while using the engine to give them maximum speed. He stood at the wheel using his binoculars to gauge the distance between the catamaran and the other boat.

Gil didn't need to use anything but his own eyes to see the boat was gaining on them. That last bullet was too close for comfort, Gil thought, looking at the way the railing on the boat dimpled before the bullet had ricocheted out to sea. They had a lot of sail up for Sanchez's men to use as a target. One bullet hole could slice the sail in two, causing the boat to lose speed and have both Gil and Sonny's dad reeling to control the damage.

It'd be all over then.

"How far out is the Coast Guard?"

"About ten minutes."

At the helm, Sonny's father grumbled. "They're going to be ten minutes too late if we don't pick up some speed. Come take the wheel. I'm getting the other rifle."

Gil got his first close glimpse of the approaching boat through the binoculars. Two rifles against the fire-power he saw coming at them wasn't going to be enough. But he wasn't prepared to give up.

"If there are more bullets, get them, too. We're going to need them."

Deep sobs racked Sonny's body as she listened to the gunfire above her. Her father's shouts intermingled with Gil's. She knew they were both exposed to bullets that were being fired at them from the other boat, and it was more than she could bear.

The sound of a helicopter in the distance began to grow louder. Within minutes, the noise of it was so pronounced, it scared Ellie and she started to cry for the first time since the ordeal started. The helicopter wasn't directly above the boat but it sounded as if it were circling them.

"This is the United States Coast Guard," Sonny heard loud and clear. "Heave to and prepare to be boarded."

A surge of relief consumed Sonny. The United States Coast Guard was here—finally.

The command to heave to was repeated, followed by

the cut of the engine. The catamaran lost its speed and instead of cutting through the water it was floating.

"We're almost home, Ellie! Almost home."

"You're still in international waters," the Coast Guard lieutenant said. "Our being here was enough to chase them off, but we can't guarantee they won't come back once we fly out of here. There's a cutter patrolling the waters on the outskirts of Puerto Rico. I've radioed for them to come out and escort you the rest of the way. They should meet you by the end of the day. If you run into trouble before you rendezvous with the cutter, make sure you radio us again."

The lieutenant and a Coast Guard crewman had boarded the catamaran after the boat chasing them took flight in the opposite direction.

"I appreciate your help. I thought we were done for," Gil said.

"You say you logged your trip when you left port," the lieutenant asked Sonny's father.

"Yes, you'll find it on file. I'm bringing three more passengers back with me. They all have their passports on board."

The lieutenant nodded. "I'll make note of that for our log, but you'll need to check in with Immigration and the Coast Guard office in Ponce as soon as you dock, Mr. Montgomery. You'll need to file a report."

"Will do. Thank you again."

As the Coast Guard crew lifted to the helicopter and flew off, Gil turned to Sonny's father. "You look tired, sir."

He was met with a scowl on the older man's face.

"Let's cut it with the 'sir,' shall we? My name is Kelin. Kelly to my friends."

"So where does that leave me?"

He heaved a sigh. "I'm still deciding. Seeing how my daughter has taken a liking to you despite the mess you put her in, I'm thinking Kelly would be okay. Unless you only mean to use her for your own profit. In which case, you won't be calling me anything."

"I care a great deal for Sonny."

Kelly propped his hands on his hips. "And still you almost had her killed. And my granddaughter."

"I can't change that. If I could, I would. But I didn't do it entirely on my own. From what Sonny has told me, she put herself in this position willingly despite your reservations and Dylan's."

Surprise registered on his face. "She told you about her brother, huh?"

"She's talked openly about them both. She loves them very much."

"That she does." He paused a moment and looked hard at Gil. "You a praying man, Gil?"

He could lie and say yes, but he didn't really want to start his relationship with Sonny's father on that note. "I wasn't always. But it seems that's all I've been doing lately."

Kelly nodded. "Worrying about loved ones can take a lot out of a man."

Gil had been the cause of Kelly's worry for at least one of his loved ones, he decided. Judging by the worry lines on Kelly's face, Gil figured he wasn't going to let him off the hook easily. Even after the blow he'd delivered earlier.

"How's the jaw?" Kelly asked.

"Sore, but I'll survive."

"If I'd really wanted to hurt you I would have. And believe me, there were times over the past week when I wanted to."

Gil had no doubt. Despite the terse words from Kelly, he'd calmed some in the past few minutes, and then he surprised Gil by chuckling.

"It wasn't a very Christian way to behave, I'm afraid," Kelly said, with a shake of his head. "My wife would be appalled. She can deliver her own left hook without even touching me, though, when she's displeased by something I've done. And she'd be displeased about this, especially seeing the way Sonny feels about you."

Gil blinked. "I'm sorry, sir?"

"Are we back to that already?" Kelly said, scowling.

Gil shrugged.

Kelly eyed him speculatively. "You be careful with Sonny. No matter how much she's grown into a woman, she's still my little girl and I'm not going to let you hurt her."

"I don't think you have to worry. We've been at odds a fair amount of the time we've spent together." Well, that wasn't completely true, but they had argued.

Kelly chuckled, lifting his eyes skyward. "Lord, I'm in trouble with this one. He's clueless."

A frown pulled at Gil's face.

"You might not have had the opportunity to figure it out yet, but my little girl doesn't pay much mind to men she doesn't like. I don't mean she's impolite. That's not Sonny's way. But if you got her riled up, she's seeing something in you." Kelly pointed a finger at Gil. "Remember what I said, and watch yourself. I don't want my little girl hurt."

Gil smiled. "You have my word."

Kelly made a grunt. "Well, you got her back to me. And with my grandbaby, too. That says something. I guess I can't ask for more than that from the Lord."

Despite his initial reaction to Gil, it was easy to see where Sonny's strong faith came from. More than a few times Gil had looked in Kelly's direction while they were being chased. He talked openly to the Lord as if He were a passenger on this vessel along with the rest of them.

But then, Gil supposed He was. He wasn't going to question how Kelly had managed to reach them before Eduardo Sanchez did, or how the Coast Guard had found them just in time to scare off their pursuers.

Kelly pointed to the captain's wheel. "What do you know about navigating a catamaran?"

Gil gave him a grin. "Enough to keep her true while you go introduce yourself to Ellie and have a real look. She's a sweetheart."

That earned him a beaming smile from Kelly. "I hear she's the spitting image of my wife, too."

"Sonny?"

"Back here, Dad!" she called out. She'd found some baby supplies in one of the cabinets and changed Ellie's diaper. Serena must have stocked the boat before her father set sail.

Kelly poked his head into the berth. "There're my girls." His laugh of joy was loud; it startled Ellie and had her twisting around in Sonny's arms to see the source of the noise.

"Well, I'll be. She does look like your mother," her dad said, tears filling his eyes. "You're a breath of fresh air, little one."

Sonny blinked back her own tears. "Here. Why don't you hold her while I get her a bottle?"

Ellie looked lost in her granddad's big arms. But he turned her and easily fit her into the crook of his arm like a pro.

"I'll be right back."

In her search for diapers Sonny also found some ready-made bottles of formula. She heated one and brought it back to the berth where she'd left her father and Ellie.

Her father was stretched out on the bunk. Ellie was sitting up, propped on his stomach, and he was making her laugh big belly laughs. The worry she'd seen on her dad's face had been momentarily replaced with pure contentment.

She hoped with all her heart that God would let them all have many more moments like this. She couldn't wait to get home and see that same joy on her mother's face. On Serena's face. And God willing, on Cash's face, if Dylan was successful in finding him and bringing him home.

"Did you call Serena to tell her we were coming in?" her father asked.

"You mean you didn't hear the shriek? It was the first thing I did when you were talking to the Coast Guard."

Tears filled Sonny's eyes as she watched her father

holding Ellie. If it was in God's plan, Cash would be holding her soon.

"She and Mom are going to meet us at the Coast Guard station, in Ponce."

"Good. Any word from Dylan yet?"

Sonny shook her head. "I talked to Tammie, too. She said it's still too early."

Dylan's fiancée had been in contact with Dylan only once since they'd left to rescue Cash. Although Tammie did say she was hopeful they'd hear something soon, she reminded Sonny that Dylan had warned them he would be unable to check in until he and his team had retrieved Cash and were on their way home.

Still, Sonny could not ignore the worried lines that had reappeared on her father's face. Now that they were out of danger, she got a good look at him and he appeared so much older than she remembered. It was as if he had aged ten years in a matter of weeks.

"Worry over your kids will do it to you," he said, reading her mind. "Go. You don't have to babysit me. Ellie is fine."

Her mouth dropped open. "I wasn't suggesting she wasn't."

"I know. But you have that does-he-know-what-he's-doing look about you. I may be a grandpa for the first time but I managed to raise three children to adulthood. I do know a thing or two about babies."

She offered him a smile. "Yeah, I guess you did a pretty good job at that."

He lifted his eyes toward the stairs leading up to the deck. "What's going on, Sonny?"

A slow rise of heat flushed her face. Never in her life

had she talked about men with her father. Aside from the fact that she rarely dated, there really hadn't ever been anyone worth bringing home to meet her parents.

It had only been a few days since she met Gil, and already she was having a hard time remembering what life was like before him. What did she think about all day? Now, she seemed to be consumed with thoughts of Gil.

If this trip to Colombia had proven one thing to her family—and to herself—it was that she wasn't a little girl anymore. She wasn't going to hide what she felt from her father.

She cleared her throat. "If you're asking me if I'm in love with Gil, the answer is…I don't know. I just hope you don't judge him based on what happened in Colombia."

"He almost got you killed. And Ellie. How am I supposed to feel about that?"

"He had no idea what was going on when he stopped us at the airport. He got us out of Colombia. And he protected me when he could have been killed himself."

Her father considered her words for a minute. A sense of pride filled her as she realized he was seeing her in a new light.

He finally chuckled and gave Ellie a big kiss on the cheek, making her laugh. "If I still had any kind of pull where you're concerned, you never would've gone down to Colombia. But what an incredible mistake that would have been if we couldn't have this precious little baby back with us. I guess sometimes your dad doesn't always know what's best for you, Sonny."

Her father's face grew serious.

"But I can't ignore his possible reasons for being involved with you. He was after your brother. Just like those federal officers who wouldn't listen to the evidence. How do you know he isn't just going along for the ride to find Cash?"

"He believes in Cash's innocence."

"Is he still determined to interfere? To look for Cash? You know what that might do to both your brothers if he succeeds."

She knew full well that if Gil and his team managed to find Cash before Dylan got him out of Colombia that both her brothers—and Gil—could wind up dead.

Sonny chose her words carefully. "He knows how serious this situation is. He won't put Dylan and Cash in danger."

"I hope not. I hope whatever it is that you're seeing in him is…" Kelly stopped himself and shook his head. "You're well beyond the age where I can tell you what to do, Sonny."

"Thanks, Dad." She gave him a kiss on the cheek and smiled at Ellie, who was wiggling happily in her grandfather's arms.

Then, with a weary heart, she climbed the stairs in search of Gil. She had no idea what would happen when Gil started searching for Cash again. But she thought she was falling in love. And that was possibly the scariest thing that had happened to her since she'd come to Colombia.

FIFTEEN

Gil sat at the helm, his bare feet propped up on a storage container, his shoes in a pile on the floor next to it. He was leaning back in the captain's chair with his arms behind him and his hands entwined, resting at the nape of his neck.

He'd been deep in thought and the look on his face told Sonny she'd startled him. But his expression quickly softened when he realized it was her.

"Any word from Marco and Cooper?" Sonny asked.

Gil nodded, rubbing his jaw, which probably ached after the punch her father had given him. "Safely back in the States."

"I'm sorry for the way my father treated you," she said, settling in the chair on the other side of the deck.

"That's okay. It's not like he didn't have reason. I probably would have decked me, too, if I were him."

Sonny could relax a bit, knowing Ellie was downstairs with her father. He was enjoying some grandpa time with his first grandchild, giving Sonny her first opportunity since they'd met to let her guard down around Gil.

She didn't have to be in control anymore. There were two strong men on board that could take that lead for her.

"How's the jaw?" she asked. She winced inside—opening up a can of worms about her father hitting him might not be the wisest way to start.

Gil moved his jaw back and forth as if to test it. "I'll survive."

Sonny wondered if her heart would.

"I'm sorry. My family is a bit overprotective of me."

With the sun setting behind him, he looked incredibly handsome.

"You don't have to apologize," he said, frowning.

"Yes, I kinda have to."

"You didn't punch me."

"You're not likely to get a warm reception from Dylan, either," she said, biting her bottom lip. "So, it's kind of an apology in advance."

His eyes widened for a fraction of a second and then he laughed. She could barely hear it over the sound of the water rushing against the side of the catamaran and the fluttering of the sails in the breeze.

"I guess that's to be expected. Good news is I just got word from the Coast Guard cutter that we should be reaching Ponce by midday tomorrow," Gil said. "You'll finally be on United States soil."

Tears that she had held back for so long finally surged to the surface. Instantly, she felt Gil beside her, his strong arms wrapped around her.

"Are you always this much of a mess with good news?" he teased.

Sonny laughed through her tears. "I guess it's all just hitting me now."

"You mean it's taken this long? It hit me pretty fierce back in the square when I saw those guns pointed at us." He brushed her hair away from her face and leaned forward. "You're driving me crazy, Sonny. And I want to kiss you again. Will your father shoot me if I do?"

She rolled her eyes at him. "Don't be silly. He won't shoot you." Then she chuckled. "He'll just *feel* like shooting you."

"Then I guess I'm safe."

"As safe as we're going to be until this is all over and Cash is home."

He tipped her chin up with his fingers so she was looking directly at him. He had the most extraordinary eyes and if she hadn't been so terrified at the airport, it would've been the first thing she noticed about him.

Gil gazed at Sonny and wondered how he'd been lucky enough to find a woman so incredible and so alive. How had he wandered aimlessly through his life not knowing her?

He'd spent many years with Special Forces in the military and the past seven chasing criminals. He was a nomad by nature, not a family man, and yet something about being with Sonny made him think he'd cheated himself out of the best part of life.

She felt good in his arms, as if God made it so that a man had only one perfect fit and Sonny was his.

He kissed her gently and then with more intensity. When their lips parted, he held her for a long time and said a silent prayer of thanks to the Lord for guiding him in this direction, helping him find his way to Sonny.

Listening to the sounds of the water sloshing against

the catamaran as it cut its way through the Caribbean Sea, a distressing thought invaded the quiet tranquility he'd been feeling.

"He's never going to forgive me for putting you in danger, is he?"

"I don't know. My father might be a bit…ornery at times, but he's a fair man."

"No, he won't."

Sonny turned in his arms to look at him. "How do you know that?"

"Because I wouldn't if I were in his shoes."

"Even if you knew what he knows?"

"Which is?"

"That I'm falling in love with you." Her voice cracked as she said the words. "At least, it feels that way. I can't know for sure because I've never been in love before. Not like this."

Her bottom lip was quivering and he wanted more than anything to put his mouth on hers and just die with her in his arms.

But her face changed and her eyes turned cloudy. "I won't lie to you. I don't know how my father is going to feel when we get to Ponce. Right now he's in pure bliss holding his granddaughter. But I don't know if that joy will be enough to erase what he's been feeling for the past week. Or the last few months for that matter."

He nodded. "I appreciate your honesty."

"It's important to me that you care about this. I care a lot about you."

"I feel the same." He bent forward to kiss her but she pulled back, putting her hand on his chest.

"But we can't entirely trust what we're feeling."

Puzzled, he leaned away from her to get a good look at her face. She was serious.

"You can't say that what's happened to us is at all normal in any way. These feelings might not be real."

Gil's insides ached just hearing her say the words.

"Let's be realistic," she said. "Our emotions have been on edge since the moment we met. Under the circumstances, how can we really know that what we're feeling is genuine?"

"What are you saying to me?"

She sighed. "I'm not sure. This has all been so fast and so much has happened in the last month—week, even—that I'm not sure which end is up. All I'm saying is that I think we need to slow down a little and think about what is really going on with us."

"And this has nothing to do with my going after your brother? Bringing him in when he's found?"

He couldn't read her expression. "I'm saying that we need to slow down."

"You still think this is all about money?"

"It's not about Cash or what you are going to do. It's about how we feel."

"Why don't I believe that? When you were kissing me just now, there was no hesitation, no uncertainty. Why now? What changed? Are you sure you're not afraid of your family's reaction to me?"

She shook her head. "I should be—they're very protective of me. But my father seemed open to it earlier. And Dylan, well, he'll behave. I hope."

Despite the warning Sonny was giving him, Gil couldn't help but think he'd like her older brother.

"I'm just saying, let's wait and see how we feel when we get back to Puerto Rico," she said.

"You say you know how you feel about me, but I wonder if that's true," he countered.

Her eyes filled with tears. "Let's just wait and see." Then she went below, leaving him on deck to watch the Caribbean sunset alone.

Despite her reservations, Gil knew the feelings between Sonny and him were real. More real than anything he'd ever experienced in his life. If she needed time, he'd give it to her.

She was still scared. She had been through a lot and needed to rely on her family right now. That much was for certain. He wished he could tell her that as long as she leaned on him, too, they'd be okay.

Sonny could hardly contain herself that morning when she looked out the portal and saw the shoreline of Puerto Rico. United States soil never looked so good. The Coast Guard cutter was dead ahead of them, leading the way.

Ellie was talking to herself, stretching her legs and waving her arms wildly in the little crib Serena had put on board. It was almost as if she knew she was going to see her mommy again.

Unable to stay cooped up in the little bunk, Sonny quickly jumped out of bed and yanked on a pair of jeans and an oversized T-shirt.

"You're going to see your mommy, sweet pea," she said, nuzzling Ellie's belly as she changed her into a fresh diaper and clothes. Gil was already on deck with her father, who was at the helm radioing the harbormaster to announce their arrival.

Lifting the baby into her arms, Sonny quickly walked through the main cabin and climbed the stairs to the deck.

"Your mother is going to be there when we dock," her father said, sitting at the wheel. His face grew bright at the sight of Ellie. "She's going to love this little one."

A bubble of laughter escaped Sonny, which made Ellie giggle, too.

"The cutter just radioed. They want us to file a report about what happened, and then check in with Customs before going to the Immigration office so they can validate our passports," Gil said.

"You still have Ellie's?" Kelly asked.

"I have it downstairs," Sonny replied, searching the dock for familiar faces. "We're all set."

"Then we're home free. For this leg of the journey, anyway," Kelly said.

Just as planned, Sonny's mother was standing at the pier with Serena and Tammie. Tears blurred her eyes as she held Ellie in her arms, waiting for the boat to dock and for Serena to climb on board. There wasn't a dry eye among them when Sonny handed Ellie over to Serena.

"My goodness! You've gotten so big, Ellie," Serena cried. "Oh, my sweetheart. I can't believe I'm holding you. Thank you for bringing her home to me, Sonny." Ellie seemed confused by all the commotion around her. It would take a few days for the strangeness to wear off but Sonny was sure mother and daughter would bond again as if the past few months had never happened.

Sonny turned to her mother and gave her a hug.

"Thank you, God, for bringing my daughter back

to me," her mother whispered. "What happened to you in Colombia?"

Sonny kissed her mother's cheek. "It's a long story, Mom."

Then, she turned to Tammie, who had her arms outstretched, ready to give her a hug. "It's good to have you back, Sonny," Tammie said.

Almost afraid to ask, Sonny hesitated. "Any word from Dylan yet?"

Her smile became brighter, if that was at all possible given the reunion taking place on the dock. "The troops are coming home."

Her pulse pounded. "All of them?"

"That's right! A bit rough around the edges but otherwise able."

Sonny closed her eyes and gave praise to the Lord for seeing them all through this journey that seemed like a never ending nightmare. She was almost afraid to laugh through her tears for fear that someone would take the joy away.

Serena could hardly talk, she was so overcome. Pressing Ellie's cheek against her face, she said, "My family is almost complete."

"Don't you worry," Kelly said. "Dylan will have Cash back to you soon. Then we can all celebrate Montgomery-style!"

"That's sounds wonderful."

In the midst of all the commotion, Sonny had lost track of Gil. She looked around the dock and saw him off on the sidelines.

"Did you hear that, Gil? Cash is coming home!" She launched herself into his arms, despite Gil's confused expression. "I can't believe it. My brothers are coming home."

He held on to her.

"It feels strange not having Ellie in my arms now that she's back with Serena," Sonny said.

"She's safe with her mom. And she's not going anywhere. You're going to get to enjoy being her auntie for the rest of your life."

"It'll be nice not to have to look over my shoulder. To just enjoy her, you know?"

"Yeah."

She pulled back to look at his expression. "What's wrong? You're sad."

He shook his head. "Come here with me."

Gil took her by the hand and pulled her with him to the deck of the catamaran.

"What are you doing?"

"I want to talk to you." He drew in a deep breath and pulled her into his arms. "I've been thinking of what you said last night."

She placed her hands on his face. "We don't have to discuss that now. Nothing needs to be decided."

"I think it does."

Her heart dropped. "I don't want to argue about this, Gil."

"Some people might call it communicating," he said. His eyes smiled but his face was serious. "I sat right here holding you close and feeling like there was nowhere else I wanted to be than on this boat with you in my arms."

She studied his face. She saw light and hope there. He meant what he said.

Sonny sighed. "But what if it's not real, Gil?"

"My feelings for you couldn't get any more real than this," he said quietly. The wind blew his hair around his face. Dark eyes that seemed determined and gentle at the same time peered into hers.

The lines that made deep crevasses around his eyes suddenly smoothed away and turned into a full smile. "I love you. I don't want this to be the end for us. I can't change what happened in Colombia any more than you can. And I take my job seriously. When Cash gets back, I need to bring him in."

She swallowed. "I can't let you do that, Gil—he's my brother. They'll kill him. If they didn't kill him in Colombia, they'll do it in jail."

A tear ran down her cheek.

"I won't let that happen."

She continued through her tears. "You don't have the power to stop it. You saw what Eduardo Sanchez and his people can do."

"I know he's innocent. Neither Dylan nor I are going to allow him to be in harm's way. If I have to guard him with my life, I will. And I'm going to do everything in my power to help Cash get the charges against him dropped."

Her eyes widened. "You'd do that for him?"

"I'd do it for you. For us."

She wrapped her arms around him tighter, unable to believe God had blessed her by bringing this amazing man into her life. "Thank you, Lord," she whispered.

He released her gently and looked around the dock at Sonny's family. "My way of life has had me living like a nomad for years. But I've been thinking."

"Yes?"

"I need a change. I've managed to save some money, enough for me to take time off, maybe reevaluate my options."

She nodded. "Oh. Where will you go?"

He gave her a half grin. "Don't you worry. It won't be far from you."

She smiled and kissed him.

Then he looked around. "Do you like this boat?"

Confusion filled her. "It's nice."

He took a deep breath, as if he needed to draw strength. Then he cleared his throat and looked directly at her. "Look, I'm going to ask you something and I want you to think about it for a while. You know, give yourself time until this whole thing with Cash is over and we have the people from the Aztec Corporation responsible for Cash and Ellie's kidnapping behind bars."

Sonny groaned. "That may take a while."

"Your family is not all that thrilled with me right now."

"They'll get over it."

"I don't want that to be a source of distress for you, Sonny. I'm not blaming them for the way they feel. I know I'd feel the same if the situation was reversed."

She shook her head, not sure what he was getting at. "You're my choice, Gil. Not theirs."

He smiled. "I want to marry you, Sonny. I know it sounds crazy, but I know what I feel and—"

She launched herself into his arms and silenced him with a kiss. When she pulled back, she looked into his stunned eyes. "I'm sorry for what I said last night, Gil. I can't believe I questioned our feelings for each other."

Gil spun her around on deck. "You're amazing. I think I've loved you since that very first kiss at the airport."

"Gil, you haven't seen anything yet." She laughed and kissed him again.

"Good. What do you think about taking this boat out for our honeymoon? I've been wanting some downtime, maybe go scuba diving—"

She threw her head back and laughed. "I've never been."

"I can teach you or we can take a class so you can get certified. Maybe find some sunken ships in the Caribbean."

"Buried treasure?"

"As long as I'm with you, I don't need any other treasure, Sonny."

She nuzzled his neck. "A honeymoon on the Caribbean, huh?"

"We can just enjoy being together. No pirates to worry about or needing to call the Coast Guard for a rescue."

"Oh, I know I won't have to worry about any of that."

"Why?"

"Because you'll be there to protect me. What more could I possibly need?"

In his arms, Sonny truly felt blessed. Blessed to be home and to have the love of a man she knew was a gift from God.

* * * * *

Dear Reader,

I was pleasantly overwhelmed by the e-mails I received from people who read *Cradle of Secrets* and fell in love with Cash, Serena and Ellie as much as I did. I was thrilled to be able to write this next installment, *Her Only Protector,* so you all could reconnect with familiar characters and find out what happened to them.

In *Her Only Protector,* Sonny needs to rely on her faith and the strength she derives from her family to overcome situations that most of us will never know. As I wrote the story of Ellie's rescue, I thought of different situations in my life where my family and my faith became the rock in my life that grounded me.

I'm currently writing the last story in the series about Cash and Serena's reunion. To find out more about upcoming books, contests and general news, please check out my Web site www.lisamondello.com or visit www.ladiesofsuspense.blogspot.com.

I so enjoyed getting your e-mails and letters. Please keep in touch at lisamondello@aol.com.

Many blessings to you all,

Lisa Mondello

QUESTIONS FOR DISCUSSION

1. Kidnapping is a serious charge. How does Sonny use her faith to come to grips with "kidnapping" Ellie?

2. Sonny needs to travel to a foreign country to rescue her niece. She's all alone, without her family. How does she use the knowledge that her family loves her—and her faith—to get her through her ordeal?

3. Trust is a huge part of any relationship. Right from the beginning, Sonny needs to trust Gil, but she struggles with how much she should trust him when he clearly wants to use her to find Cash. How does Sonny deal with issues of trust throughout the story?

4. Lucia was killed during Ellie's rescue. How does Sonny use her faith to deal with her guilt over Lucia's death?

5. There are times throughout the story that Sonny needed to lie to keep Ellie safe. Have you ever had to lie to protect someone? How did it make you feel?

6. Gil grapples with why he distanced himself from his faith in God. He admits that there was no particular event other than his mother's grief over her sister's death that could explain it. Has there ever

been a time in your life when you found yourself distant from your faith? If so, what brought you back?

7. People pray at different times and for different reasons. Sonny sees Gil in the courtyard alone and thinks he's "talking to the moon." She's surprised when she realizes later that she'd wrongly assumed he wasn't a faithful man. Have you ever made the mistake of assuming a person is not faithful because they are not open about their faith?

8. Gil clearly feels responsible for preventing Sonny and Ellie from getting on the plane to the United States. Have you ever done something that put someone else in danger? How did you use your faith to deal with the responsibility of that?

9. Sonny fears that her family won't approve of Gil. Her father is clearly wary of her being involved with a person who put her life in danger and was after Cash. How does Sonny come to terms with this?

10. Gil was clearly affected by the death of his former partner. He also admits that he's good at his job and makes a lot of money, but then feels as if his greed for money might have clouded his judgment. Do you think Gil is right?

11. After just a week of being together, Gil realized he wants to be with Sonny. Do you think that two people can be that certain of their love that soon?

12. Sonny tells Gil that her faith is the backbone of her life and her family's life. She's dealing with extraordinary circumstances that could lead to her death and to the death of her niece. Do you think her strong faith in God helps her get through the trials she faces in the story?

13. Sonny naturally feels protective of Ellie because of her circumstances. She has difficulty trusting the baby with the others. How did Sonny resolve those feelings?

Love Inspired
HISTORICAL
INSPIRATIONAL HISTORICAL ROMANCE

Adelaide Crum longs for a family, but the closed-minded town elders refuse to entrust even the most desperate orphan to a woman alone. Newspaperman Charles Graves promises to stand by her, despite his embittered heart. Adelaide's gentle soul soon makes him wonder if he can overcome his bitter past, and somehow find the courage to love....

Look for

Courting Miss Adelaide
by
JANET DEAN

Available September wherever books are sold, including most bookstores, supermarkets, drugstores and discount stores.

www.SteepleHill.com

Steeple
Hill®

REQUEST YOUR FREE BOOKS!

2 FREE RIVETING INSPIRATIONAL NOVELS
PLUS 2 FREE MYSTERY GIFTS

Love Inspired.
SUSPENSE

YES! Please send me 2 FREE Love Inspired® Suspense novels and my 2 FREE mystery gifts (gifts are worth about $10). After receiving them, if I don't wish to receive any more books, I can return the shipping statement marked "cancel". If I don't cancel, I will receive 4 brand-new novels every month and be billed just $4.24 per book in the U.S. or $4.74 per book in Canada, plus 25¢ shipping and handling per book and applicable taxes, if any*. That's a savings of over 20% off the cover price! I understand that accepting the 2 free books and gifts places me under no obligation to buy anything. I can always return a shipment and cancel at any time. Even if I never buy another book, the two free books and gifts are mine to keep forever.

123 IDN ERXX 323 IDN ERXM

Name	(PLEASE PRINT)	
Address		Apt. #
City	State/Prov.	Zip/Postal Code

Signature (if under 18, a parent or guardian must sign)

Order online at www.LoveInspiredSuspense.com
Or mail to Steeple Hill Reader Service:

IN U.S.A.: P.O. Box 1867, Buffalo, NY 14240-1867
IN CANADA: P.O. Box 609, Fort Erie, Ontario L2A 5X3

Not valid to current subscribers of Love Inspired Suspense books.

Want to try two free books from another series?
Call 1-800-873-8635 or visit www.morefreebooks.com

* Terms and prices subject to change without notice. N.Y. residents add applicable sales tax. Canadian residents will be charged applicable provincial taxes and GST. Offer not valid in Quebec. This offer is limited to one order per household. All orders subject to approval. Credit or debit balances in a customer's account(s) may be offset by any other outstanding balance owed by or to the customer. Please allow 4 to 6 weeks for delivery. Offer available while quantities last.

Your Privacy: Steeple Hill Books is committed to protecting your privacy. Our Privacy Policy is available online at www.SteepleHill.com or upon request from the Reader Service. From time to time we make our lists of customers available to reputable third parties who may have a product or service of interest to you. If you would prefer we not share your name and address, please check here. □

LISUS08R

Love Inspired®
SUSPENSE

TITLES AVAILABLE NEXT MONTH

Don't miss these four stories in September

DOUBLE CROSS by Terri Reed
The McClains
Her family's orchid farm is Kiki Brill's pride and joy. She
won't sell, no matter how much Ryan McClain offers. But as
accidents threaten her peaceful life on Maui, the wealthy,
handsome businessman, once the prime suspect, begins to
seem like her last hope.

BADGE OF HONOR by Carol Steward
In the Line of Fire
Why would FBI agent Sarah Roberts start over as a small-
town cop? She *has* to be undercover. And police officer
Nick Matthews knows exactly who Sarah is spying on: him.
Then Sarah's past crashes down on them. Trusting his new
partner becomes a matter of life, death—and love.

THE FACE OF DECEIT by Ramona Richards
Karen O'Neill barely remembers her parents' murder. Still,
she's haunted by a face—which she sculpts into her vases.
Now, an art buyer is dead and Karen's vases are being
shattered. Art expert Mason DuBroc believes the clues are
in the clay. Can they decode them in time?

FINAL DEPOSIT by Lisa Harris
It's bad enough that Lindsey Taylor's father lost his savings
in an Internet scam. Now he's gone to claim his "fortune,"
and Lindsey fears she'll never see him again. Financial
security expert Kyle Walker promises to help her. But the
closer they get, the more danger they find....

LISCNM0808